THE S

THE S

LESLIE CHARTERIS

These are the titles in order of sequence
(the original titles are shown in brackets)

THE SAINT MEETS THE TIGER
  (*Meet the Tiger*)
ENTER THE SAINT
THE SAINT CLOSES THE CASE
  (*The Last Hero*)
THE AVENGING SAINT
  (*Knight Templar*)
FEATURING THE SAINT
ALIAS THE SAINT
THE SAINT MEETS HIS MATCH
  (*She Was a Lady*)
THE SAINT v. SCOTLAND YARD
  (*The Holy Terror*)
THE SAINT'S GETAWAY
  (*Getaway*)
THE SAINT AND MR. TEAL
  (*Once More the Saint*)
THE BRIGHTER BUCCANEER
THE SAINT IN LONDON
  (*The Misfortunes of Mr. Teal*)
THE SAINT INTERVENES
  (*Boodle*)
THE SAINT GOES ON
THE SAINT IN NEW YORK
SAINT OVERBOARD
THE ACE OF KNAVES
THE SAINT BIDS DIAMONDS
  (*Thieves' Picnic*)
THE SAINT PLAYS WITH FIRE
  (*Prelude for War*)
FOLLOW THE SAINT
THE HAPPY HIGHWAYMAN
THE SAINT IN MIAMI
THE SAINT GOES WEST
THE SAINT STEPS IN
THE SAINT ON GUARD
THE SAINT SEES IT THROUGH
CALL FOR THE SAINT
SAINT ERRANT
THE SAINT IN EUROPE
THE SAINT ON THE SPANISH MAIN
THE SAINT AROUND THE WORLD
THANKS TO THE SAINT
SEÑOR SAINT
THE SAINT TO THE RESCUE
TRUST THE SAINT
THE SAINT IN THE SUN
VENDETTA FOR THE SAINT
THE SAINT'S CHOICE
  (Introduced by Leslie Charteris)
THE SAINT ON TV
THE FIRST SAINT OMNIBUS
THE SECOND SAINT OMNIBUS

SPANISH FOR FUN

LESLIE CHARTERIS

THE SAINT RETURNS

I THE DIZZY DAUGHTER
II THE GADGET LOVERS

HODDER PAPERBACKS

*The villains in this book are entirely imaginary
and bear no relation to any living person*

COPYRIGHT © 1967, 1968 BY LESLIE CHARTERIS
FIRST PRINTED IN GREAT BRITAIN 1969
HODDER PAPERBACK EDITION 1970

*Printed in Great Britain
for Hodder Paperbacks Limited,
St. Paul's House, Warwick Lane, London, E.C.4
by Richard Clay (The Chaucer Press), Ltd.,
Bungay, Suffolk*

SBN 340 12941 7

This book is sold subject to the condition that it shall not, by way of trade or otherwise, be lent, re-sold, hired out or otherwise circulated without the publisher's prior consent in any form of binding or cover other than that in which this is published and without a similar condition including this condition being imposed on the subsequent purchaser.

CONTENTS

	Page
Forewarning	7
I. THE DIZZY DAUGHTER	13
II. THE GADGET LOVERS	97

FOREWARNING

THE genesis of this book is exactly the same as that of my last publication, *The Saint on TV*. Therefore, to explain it to anyone who may have incredibly missed that epoch-making opus, I cannot do better than repeat the explanatory note with which it was prefaced:

When, after many years of noble and lofty-minded resistance, I finally broke down and sold the Saint to the Philistines of Television, I fear that I must have added one more argument to the armoury of the cynics who maintain that every man has his price; because I certainly got mine. It must have been a shattering blow to the countless millions who until then had thought I was perfect, even though I myself had never made that claim.

However, I did have enough remnants of probity to limit his period of bondage to two years, knowing full well the voracity of the mills which grind out the fodder for what I still regard as the mini-medium of mini-minds, and figuring that in that time, at the relentless pace of one show a week, they would have devoured the entire product of a not inactive writing lifetime, or anyway as much of it as was suitable for adaptation to filmlets of about 50 minutes without the commercial 'messages' and the pauses for what is hilariously called 'station identification'. I was resigned to the expectation that my stories would be considerably garbled and mutilated to conform either with the puerile tabus of unwritten censorships or the congenital megalomania of all moviemakers who can never resist 'improving' any literary creation that falls into their power, or both; but it had never occurred to me to allow the Saint to be projected into plots that had absolutely no connection whatsoever with anything I had ever written, and in fact any such liberties were specifically prohibited in my first contract.

Despite all the distortions and emasculations which shook up a probable majority of hitherto faithful readers of the Saint books, that first TV series was a big hit in Britain (where it was made) and many European countries, and was even fairly successful in the United States although presented in most areas at such impossible hours that only chronic insomniacs, night watchmen, or veritably fanatic fans would have caught it. Indeed, the American success was remarkable enough for NBC to become interested in putting the show on their full network, in colour, and in what is called 'prime time'—a promotion which had never before been offered to any series previously established in syndication.

The interesting situation then was that the British TV producers could not thumb out this possible plum without making a new deal with me, which would necessarily include the right to create original scripts.

Well, the cynics will recognize it as the same old story. After you've succumbed once, it is so much easier to succumb again. Especially when the bribe can be made so much fatter. And I have never pretended that I chose a career in writing without the most powerful mercenary motives.

So, after many hesitations and much tough bargaining, and not without very grave misgivings, I eventually consented.

The rest is history, of a sort. Many of the results, fulfilling my worst forebodings, were lamentable. But many of the so-called 'adaptations' of my own cherished stories were no less lamentable after the weird wizardries of television production got through with them. Some of those 'adaptations', in defiance of every contractual safeguard, had been almost unrecognizable anyhow. Some of the new original scripts were not much worse. Some were passable. And a few, to my pleasant surprise, were quite good.

Enter, next, three other Tempters. the *Saint Magazine*, which in 137 issues had just about exhausted the reservoir of Saint material, in spite of all the additions I had myself been able to make to the Saga during its existence, and my book publishers in America and Britain (to put them in alphabetical order) who had laboured so stoutly for me in my rising years but had long since been bemoaning the indolence of success, and who were perpetually pleading with me to give them new Saint books which, they guaranteed, would be hungrily lapped up by hordes of starved *aficionados* throughout the British Empire and the United States (to put them in alphabetical order). Why not, they conjointly urged, extend the Saga to include readable versions of some of the best of the televised inventions—subject, of course, to my own final editing?

The idea was interesting, and by no means unique in literature. Even aside from the notable 'Solar Pons' *pastiches* by August Derleth (of which several first appeared in the *Saint Magazine*) Sherlock Holmes himself had been perpetuated far beyond the range of Conan Doyle in several movies and innumerable radio series episodes based merely on the character and retailing episodes that Doyle never dreamed of. Barry Perowne, by arrangement with the estate of the late E. W. Hornung, continued the adventures of Raffles into modern times in a considerable number of stories (many of which were also first published in the *Saint Magazine*). Even while I was thinking it over, I heard that the heirs to the Ian Fleming copyrights were contemplating a continuation of the James Bond mythology—arrangements for which have since been concluded. If such a process could be tolerated by such a distinguished range of fictional characters, why should I reject it for the Saint?

If I had turned it down, there would still have been nothing I could do, so far as I know, to enjoin my own heirs from buying the same proposition some day—or, worse still, to prevent it being done without even any benefit to them by some later larcenist taking advantage of the privileged piracy sanctioned by the iniquitous concept of 'public domain'. But by permitting it now, besides enjoying some of the financial fruits myself, I would have one privilege which was denied to all the other authors I have cited: I could personally watch over and to a great extent control the desecration.

These original scripts, after all, were by agreement first submitted to me as synopses, on which I was permitted to make criticisms and suggestions, even if the producers did not invariably adopt them. The resulting scripts were again submitted to me, and again subjected to my comments, even though these were not always embodied in the final films. Now I would be in a position to choose, first, the scripts which did least violence to my own concept of a Saint story. Furthermore, the story-form adaptations would be made under my own direct and absolute supervision, permitting me to change and improve on the basic material in any way I thought desirable, in a possibly unique reversal of the usual system under which the film producer takes it upon himself to improve on the author. Finally, I would personally revise every page of the adaptations, making an honest effort to ensure that in style and phrase they were as fair a facsimile of my own writing as could be achieved without my doing all the work.

What you are about to read, therefore, is an interesting

and perhaps unprecedented experiment in team work. It is not, in any sense, a ghosted job, because I do not pretend to be the outright author. For these first offerings (and if they are well received there will be more) I have chosen story lines by John Kruse, whom I rate as easily the best TV scripter who has worked on the show, and the novelizations are by Fleming Lee, a promising young writer who I think will presently make a name of his own. I have done the back-seat driving, and added a few typical flourishes of my own. Obviously, the composite result is not even now exactly the way it might have been if I had written it all myself. But it is as close as any imitation is ever likely to get.

The reception of the first experiment has encouraged me to try it again. And if this re-run is received as well, there will be more. After all, everyone doesn't catch a TV series every single week, and by this method you might catch one of the better ones you might have missed. And in this presentation, you can enjoy it at any hour that suits you—and with no commercials.

1 THE DIZZY DAUGHTER

Adapted by Fleming Lee
    Original Story by D. R. Motton
    Teleplay by Leigh Vance

ONE

THE golden sun grew fat in its old age, and as it sank low over the distant Irish hills the whole countryside seemed to share in the hush of its going. There was no breeze. The birds were still, and even the stream, moving deep and slow between green banks, made scarcely a murmur. Only now and then a trout, striking at some floating insect in the shallows, would break the silence with a sudden splash whose purl quickly smoothed and silently vanished.

Simon Templar stood tall and lean by the water, his blue eyes watching the surface for signs of trout within range of his line. An ambiguous swirl downstream failed to distract him. He had chosen this pool because instinct—sharpened by a lifetime of hunting human prey, and not rarely being hunted himself—told him that in this widening of the stream would be lurking a prize worthy of his time and skill.

So he waited, poised and strong, his rod held ready.

That the man known somewhat incongruously as the Saint should be found in such peaceful surroundings was unusual. (His true character was better described by another of his informal appellations, voiced by police officers and criminals with equal unease, the Robin Hood of Modern Crime.) That such peace should last long, even in rural Kildare, half an hour's drive from Dublin, was inconceivable, for the Saint could no more escape adventure than a fish could escape its brook and stroll off across the fields, and in general he had no desire to do so.

But even a man whose natural medium is excitement occasionally wants a change of pace, and for the moment Simon Templar wanted and had found it—though his sixth sense, nagging like the faintly expanding sound of a speeding car in the distance, warned him to enjoy it thoroughly now before his fated propensity for trouble swung the balance back to normal.

The Saint had driven into Dublin on the previous afternoon with the plan of meeting an old friend, the soldier of fortune, Patrick Kelly, at the Gresham Hotel, spending the night there, while Kelly enjoyed a reunion with comrades-at-arms, and then going out to Kelly's house in the country seventy miles west for two or three days of fishing.

All had gone as planned up to and including Kelly's enjoyment of his reunion, in which he had insisted Simon take part. But Kelly's enjoyment had been so immense, and celebrated with such grand libations of porter and thrice-distilled Gaelic fire, that he had found himself disinclined to go on with the rest of the schedule when Simon wakened him by house phone at noon. He had found himself unready, in fact, to leave his hotel bed, and had announced in that brief interval between prolonged periods of unconsciousness that the drive to his cottage would have to be delayed at least until evening—and since they would be paying for another night in the hotel anyway, probably until the next morning.

The Saint, after a one p.m. brunch, had gone on out into the country for two reasons: he was in the mood for fishing, and he did not want to spend the afternoon near the hotel, where he would almost inevitably get involved in somebody else's problems. Among Pat Kelly's more exuberant activities of the night before, once he got to the table-pounding stage, had been the repeated proud bellowing of Simon's name not only in the Cocktail Bar of the

Gresham but also in numerous other places along the streets of Dublin's fair city. Such widespread advertising of the Saint's presence was a virtual guarantee that he would not have been able to spend an afternoon in town undisturbed by some stranger.

Near the centre of the stream the surface swirled, and a slowly waving tail broke the orange-gold reflections of overhanging trees. The Saint made a perfect cast upstream of the fish. The brightly coloured fly drifted with the current towards the target of concentric ripples made by the trout's rising, and Simon carefully reeled in just enough of the floating line to ensure control if the big fish struck.

The sound of the fast-moving car which a few moments before had been almost imperceptible was now much closer. Tyres squealed less than two hundred yards away. The only road in the vicinity followed the stream where Simon was fishing, and he was standing within thirty feet of a sharp curve in the roadway. He was not worried about his own safety, however, but about his car, which was parked on the shoulder between road and stream and could easily be demolished if the speeder overshot the turn.

Irish country roads are not made for fast travel. Cars are few, carts and sheep are plentiful, and a normal brisk driving speed is thirty-five miles per hour. So it was particularly irritating to Simon that some maniac had chosen this stretch of asphalt on which to attempt suicide, and that the aberration had to occur just when a rising trout begged for all his concentration.

Once the racing car hit the curve, there was nothing Simon could do but jerk the fly from the very mouth of the expectant fish and prepare to dodge a hurtling ton of metal. It was a green Volkswagen, and it skidded with an anguished howl of scorching rubber, rear end swinging as the driver narrowly missed Simon's car by slamming on brakes and heading for the old stone wall on the opposite side of the road. Then to avoid smashing into the wall the driver made an immediate sudden turn back towards the outside of the curve. The Volkswagen pirouetted completely around on all four wheels as if it had been on ice, miraculously failed to turn over, left the road, and skidded towards the stream, its locked rear wheels ploughing up turf, and came to a halt between two trees without hitting either.

As Simon strode towards it, his rod still in hand, the engine was dead, and the driver, a girl, was slumped forward over the wheel. But, before he had covered half the distance between them, she looked up suddenly with terror in her eyes, and it was obvious that she had been shaken rather than knocked unconscious.

She was young—scarcely nineteen, Simon estimated on first sight—and the deep brown eyes that were fixed on him were extraordinarily large. Her chestnut hair was chopped short, her mouth was small and provocative, her nose pert and uptilted.

The Saint realized instantly that neither the acrobatics of her car nor his own appearance—which considering his frame of mind probably had a rather threatening aspect— was the cause of the stark fear on her pretty face. After the initial moment of staring at him, she looked up the road in the direction from which she had come, grabbed at the door handle, and scrambled out of her car.

It was then that Simon heard the second car rushing nearer, with the same screech of tyres on curves which had preceded the arrival of the girl, and realized that it was the apparent cause of her panic.

'Le Mans is that way,' he said helpfully, gesturing with his fishing rod. 'You must have missed a turn somewhere.'

'Please!' she cried. 'Help me!'

She was hurrying towards him, the short tight skirt of her stylish suit restricting her legs, her stiletto heels stabbing into the damp earth of the stream's bank.

'Help you do what?' he asked. 'Change tyres for the next stretch? I'm sorry, but I don't have much sympathy for anybody who...'

'They'll get me,' she gasped, stumbling up to him and clutching his arms. 'Hide me. Do something.'

She was a foot shorter than the Saint, and had to look almost straight up to meet his sceptical blue eyes at that close range.

'This reminds me of a movie I saw once,' he said blandly. 'Except there the girl kissed the stranger and said, "Please don't look up—hold me!" and then along came...'

The girl interrupted him with a despairing wail as a second car—this one a black Mercedes—came around the curve at a slightly saner rate than her Volkswagen had done, put on its brakes, and skidded to a stop on the road. Then it backed up with a roar and a spinning of wheels on to the shoulder between her car and Simon's.

'Do something!' she begged, putting the Saint between her and the emerging occupants of the Mercedes, and grasping his arms more tightly than ever.

'I'd have a better chance if my hands were free,' he told her.

As she let him go and cowered by the water, the two men who had been in the black car sized up the situation and began moving slowly forward, separating to divide Simon's attention and cut down possible routes for his and the girl's escape. One of the quietly methodical and confident-seeming pursuers was rather overweight for his job, and his tautly stretched trench coat looked as if it had seen better days on a slenderer version of him. His bald dome gleamed red in the setting sun.

The second man was considerably smaller, and his trench coat was more rumpled than stretched. Greying sandy hair was closely cropped on his narrow head, and veins showed large around his temples. His tongue, like a snake's, continuously darted out to touch his thin lips.

Since they did not speak, Simon saw no need to initiate a conversation. He waited, relaxed and alert, and almost imperceptibly stripped line from his reel. Finally, when the men were within ten feet of him, he flicked the fly into the air, dropped it over the fat man's shoulder, and deftly sank the hook into his neck.

As the fat one yowled and groped with both hands behind him, his companion, thinking he was catching the Saint off guard, made an ill-considered move. He charged forward as Simon bent the fishing rod nearly double and let go the tip just in time to catch the attacker across the throat with the full force of the hissing whiplash of supple fibreglass.

The thin man went down on his knees, choking, and Simon simply shoved him with one strong hand into the deep stream. The obese member of the partnership, taking advantage of momentary slackness in the line, seemed about to free himself, but Simon reeled in, tugged, and brought the man wincing and stumbling forward. It was an easy matter to step out of his plump victim's path and add to the man's momentum with a swift boot to his ample rear. The splash of his belly-flop into the stream drenched the bank for yards around.

'Run!' the girl cried.

'It doesn't really seem necessary,' said the Saint, placidly winding in his freed line as he watched the men struggle in the water as the current carried them slowly downstream. 'Do you think they can swim?'

The girl glared at the sputtering pair with remarkable ferocity on her pixy face.

'I hope not!'

Simon gave her an inquiring look.

'They're *killers*,' she said.

'Not very good at it, are they?'

The girl was all but jumping up and down in her agitation.

'How can you stand there?' she whimpered. 'They're getting out. They'll murder me. Please get me away from here.'

The two men, safely out of range of Simon's fly rod, were clawing at the bank, trying to haul themselves out. The Saint was more than ready to take them on again, but he began to feel that the girl was actually going to collapse in hysterics if he did not humour her.

'All right,' he said. 'Let's go.'

From the passenger seat of his car she pleaded with him to hurry as he snatched the key from the ignition of the Mercedes, and threw it out into the stream, bringing to an abrupt halt the efforts of the swimmers to get out of the water. They went splashing towards the spot where the key had gone down. Simon leisurely clamped his rod on the roof rack of his car. (He had carried no creel, since he had no way of using fish at the moment, and had released the ones he had caught.) Then he plucked a burr from his trouser leg, slipped into the driver's seat, and started the engine, much to the relief of his passenger.

'Where to?' he asked as he turned around his car and headed for Dublin. 'Not that I'll take you there, but I'm curious to know where you'd choose if you had a choice.'

The girl sank back in the seat, letting her head loll and her mouth open to take a deep breath.

'It doesn't matter,' she sighed. 'Anywhere. I'm just so glad to get away.'

'How about Dublin?' he asked.

'That's fine.' She looked dramatically with half-closed eyes at the twilit sky ahead. 'Maybe there I can ... lose myself in the crowds.'

'Lose yourself in the crowds?' Simon repeated.

'Yes, it's my only chance. And then later, maybe, if they haven't caught up with me, I could...'

'Why don't you start from the beginning?' the Saint put in as her words faded in mid-sentence.

'I ... I can't tell it,' she said. 'If you knew, your life would be in danger too.'

'For all they know, I *do* know,' said Simon. 'So as long as my life is in danger anyway, I might as well have the satisfaction of being told why.'

'Oh, that's true!' she exclaimed, clutching his arm. 'I'm so sorry, Mr. ... I don't even know your name.'

'It's no secret,' said Simon, and he told her.

She showed no recognition.

'I'm sorry I got you into this, Mr. Templar, and I don't know how to thank you enough. I don't even have any money now. I left my purse in the car.'

Simon gave her a teasing look.

'Shall we go back and get it?'

'Oh, no!' she said. 'There ... wasn't much anyway.'

'I think the best thing to do,' the Saint said more seriously, 'is to stop at the next village and put in calls to the police and a towing service ... But we'll have to explain...'

She grabbed his arm again, shaking her head violently.

'We can't do that. For one thing ... that car ... wasn't mine.'

'Whose is it?'

'I don't know. I borrowed it.'

'Stole it?' Simon asked.

'Yes, in Carlow. It was the first one I found with a key in it—after I got away.'

Simon stopped at the Kildare–Dublin highway, turned on to it, and picked up speed—just in case Thin and Fat had retrieved their key.

'Got away from what?' he asked.

The girl sighed.

'It's such a long story, and you'll never believe it.'

'Well, give me a try. For a start, what's your name?'

'My real one?' she asked.

'Preferably,' said the Saint drily.

'You'd never believe that, either.'

He shrugged.

'I do have a nasty perverse habit of never believing people's names, but don't let that stop you.'

She hesitated.

'I'm called ... Mildred. And ...'

'And?' Simon said encouragingly.

'And my father was Adolf Hitler.'

TWO

IT was one of Simon Templar's characteristics that no blow to his mental equilibrium, however severe, was allowed to produce more than a ripple on his surface. So when his passenger announced that she was Hitler's daughter, and looked at him timorously to see what his reaction would be, she saw nothing but the usual imperturbable nonchalance.

'I'm pleased to meet you, Miss Hitler,' he said, as it occurred to him that he had possibly, just a few minutes before, deposited two employees of a mental hospital in a tributary of the River Liffey.

But that was only a passing thought, since men in white jackets, even when not wearing their white jackets, would not close menacingly in on an uninformed bystander without a word of explanation.

'I knew you wouldn't believe me,' the girl said, and she began to cry.

'Who said I didn't believe you?' protested the Saint with elaborate innocence. 'Why shouldn't I believe you?'

She sniffled, wiping her eyes with the backs of her hands. It was growing dark now, and the increasing traffic glared with headlights.

'You believe me?' she asked.

'I didn't say that, exactly. I said why shouldn't I believe you? What else can I do? I was going to suggest that when we got to my hotel we could telephone your parents, but I guess that's out of the question.'

She looked at him indignantly.

'You're callous,' she said. 'Making fun of an orphan.'

Simon, because he was driving, could not devote a really effective squelching look to her.

'Now listen to me, young lady,' he said with impressive firmness. 'I am not making fun of you. I have not even questioned your fantastic identity. I have lost a world-record trout because of you, scuffed my shoe kicking your enemies into the river, and am now in the process of further saving your neck. So if you start pulling female temperament on me, I'm going to lose patience and give you a spanking.'

She stared at him, her big eyes getting rounder.

'*Spanking?*' she squeaked.

'Yes. You look very spankable, and just the right size to fit across my knee. And I can't say I wouldn't enjoy it ... for more reasons than one.'

With compressed lips, she smiled in spite of herself.

'I'm too old for a spanking,' she said without defiance.

'Not you,' said the Saint. 'Let's see, your father died in 1945. That makes you about ... twenty-two at the least.'

'Twenty-three,' she said.

'Before we go any more into your earlier history, tell me something: why are those men trying to kill you?'

She shook her head.

'Oh. They weren't. They were trying to capture me.'

'You said they were killers.'

'Well, that wasn't exactly the truth. I couldn't tell you the whole story right then, and I had to make you take me away in a hurry, so that seemed the best thing to say.'

Simon nodded.

'Who are they, then?' he asked.

'They're SS men. They slipped into Ireland on a submarine with me during the last weeks of the war. There **were** four originally, sworn just to protect me, but one died and another one killed himself when somebody discovered his real identity.'

'And where have you been all this time—since the end of the war?'

'In a convent. And those men have lived nearby on a little farm.'

'What did the nuns think about all this?' Simon asked, slowing as Emmet Road took them in towards the heart of Dublin.

'Only the Mother Superior knew who I really was. She was a close relative of one of the high party members—the Nazi Party, I mean. The other nuns were given the story that I was the illegitimate daughter of a bishop.'

Simon covered his mouth with one hand and appeared to cough.

'The illegitimate daughter of a bishop?' he repeated, solemnly, more for confirmation of the sound than as a question.

'Yes. But I wasn't to be raised as a nun. That way I'd have been lost to the world forever. Instead I was given my own little apartment—if you can call it that—in a wing of the convent. What a lonely life that was! I had tutoring, and all the books I wanted...'

'And nice clothes,' the Saint said, glancing at her fashionable suit.

'Oh ... this? I bought this after they took me out. In fact that's how I gave them the slip. I was in the changing room of the shop to try it on, and I discovered a way out the back. So then I went along an alley to the main street and borrowed that Volkswagen. Unfortunately they realized I was taking too long and came after me, and I never managed to shake them completely.'

She was sitting bolt upright in her seat, hands folded in her lap, completely absorbed in her own words, chattering at a rate that would have shamed an auctioneer.

'Lucky thing they taught car driving at the convent,' Simon said.

She didn't bat even one eye.

'Oh, they didn't teach me there. The SS taught me on the farm. In case something happened to them they figured I might need to know how.'

'So you lived on the farm too?'

'Only for a few days, right after they took me out of the convent.'

Simon turned and crossed River Liffey between the ornate iron lamp-posts that lined either side of O'Connell Bridge.

'So here you are,' he said. 'All grown up, a skilful and sensible driver, with lots of books under your belt and lovely clothes on your lovely back. There's just one thing. Why were your guardians chasing you?'

'Because I didn't want to co-operate.'

'Co-operate in what?' Simon asked.

'Their plan is to take me back to Germany as the figurehead for a new Nazi movement.'

They had reached upper O'Connell Street and the Gresham Hotel, so Mildred's narrative had to be interrupted at the climactic point, with no really worthy response by the Saint. Surrendering the car to the doorman, he led her through the lobby, where the egress of well-clad guests for dinner, theatre, or cinema was just beginning.

'Would you like to use my room for freshening up?' Simon asked.

'I'd much rather have a drink.'

'Drinking too?' he remarked as they entered the mezzanine Cocktail Bar. 'What goes on in these convents?'

She looked at him with doe-eyed ingenuousness.

'I have to learn, don't I?'

'If it's learning to drink you want,' Simon said in a louder voice with traces of an Irish brogue, 'here's just the teacher for you.'

Patrick Kelly, who was seated at the bar attending to a bottle of Jameson, turned his great red head and split its lower half with a prognathous grin.

'Simon, ye ould dog!' he bellowed. 'Ye tould me ye were goin' fishin', but niver that this was what it was ye were fishin' for!'

'Pat, meet Mildred,' said the Saint, 'and call for two more glasses.'

Kelly gave her a more than appreciative look and his ham-sized mitt enveloped her fingers.

'I'm charmed. A face like a darlin' jewel itself she has—and here I've slept the entire mornin' away.'

'It's evening,' Mildred said innocently, taking a stool between the men.

'Oh, and shure you're mistaken,' said Kelly, rearing back to inspect the watch on his hairy wrist. 'Seven in the mornin' it must be. Here—have a bite o' breakfast.'

He poured whiskey into the clean glasses brought by the bartender. Mildred shivered and looked over her shoulder.

'What if they followed us?' she whispered.

'I wouldn't worry,' Simon said. 'And what could they do in a public place?'

'What could who do?' Kelly asked. 'Who's followin' ye?'

Simon finished his drink and stood up.

'It's a long and wonderful story, and I'll leave Mildred to tell it to you while I change for dinner. I've been fishing and fighting all afternoon.'

Kelly swelled like an excited bullfrog.

'Ye mean to say I missed a fight, too?'

'Big one,' the Saint said casually. 'SS men.'

Kelly snorted.

'Ye don't mean them big German fellas with the black uniforms? Now ye're handin' me a pail of malarkey, man. There's been none of them about for twenty years.'

'Ask Mildred,' Simon said.

As he strolled away from the bar, he heard her begin in a low confidential voice:

'How much do you remember about Hitler's death?'

When Simon returned from his room, showered and immaculately dressed, he found Kelly looking dazed and Mildred chattering like a magpie just recovered from laryngitis.

'Simon!' the Irishman exclaimed. 'Ye should only hear what she's been tellin' me!'

His sidewise look at the Saint held more doubt than his voice. He obviously wanted some confirmation or denial, but he got only a helpless gesture of upturned hands.

'Let's go eat,' Simon said. 'Mildred's problem isn't the kind of thing I like to think about with an empty stomach.'

She clutched his arm in what was becoming an habitual gesture.

'I'm frightened to go out,' she said. 'What if they . . .'

'No need to be frightened while *I'm* about,' Kelly assured her, displaying a fist big enough to crack the Blarney stone. 'Simon an' me have handled worse than a couple o' second-hand supermen.'

'And we don't even need to leave the hotel,' Simon said. 'The Grill here is as good as any place in town.'

As they were leaving the bar, Kelly stopped, tucked in his chin, and stared down at Mildred.

'But only imagine,' he said, 'a tiny thing like this going to conquer the world!'

THREE

Simon placed his fork on the platter which minutes before had been heaped with the delectable cadavers of Dublin Bay prawns, looked contentedly around at the elegant red and black décor of the Gresham Grill, and finally let his gaze come to rest on Mildred, who avoided a direct meeting with its intensity by chasing a last bit of lettuce across the salad plate. Kelly was still engaged in demolishing a double-cut steak done to dry death in the manner admired by true Gaelic countrymen.

'Mildred,' said the Saint thoughtfully, 'what are we going to do about you?'

She shrugged uncomfortably.

'I don't know. But I think I must get out of Dublin—and out of the country. I'll hide someplace where they'll never find me.' Her eyes grew brighter as inspiration began to flow again. 'I once read a story about a girl who disguised herself as a boy and signed on a ship and nobody found out for months. I'll take a schooner to the South Seas, and then I'll . . .'

Kelly looked at her figure appreciatively as he mopped his mouth with a napkin.

'I'm afraid ye'd never get away with that disguise for more than an hour.'

'No,' said Simon. 'I'm sure there must be a better way. Are you sure you've told us all the facts, exactly as they are?'

She looked him in the eye.

'As incredible as it sounds, it's all the gospel truth.'

'And I don't suppose you know anybody who can help you?' the Saint said.

'Not a soul. Only you—and I've given you too much trouble already—and put you in danger.'

She closed her eyes and tears appeared on her long brown lashes. The Saint and Kelly exchanged unbelieving but concerned glances.

'Simon,' said the Irishman, 'shure and to let her go now would be like castin' out a kitten in a snowstorm.' He pushed back his chair and gave the table a decisive thump with a meaty paw. 'If talk were cloth a man might have the makin's of an overcoat—— An ould soldier like me can't stand such a quantity of speech without no action. Here's what we'll do. We'll take her out to my place. It's so far from anything, God Himself couldn't find it with a guidebook. There she'll be safe, and Simon and me won't mind havin' a nice little girl about the house to make things cosy when we come in from fishin' all day.' He looked at Mildred. 'Me dear wife's down in Cork visitin' her mother, and I'm like a lost soul, with dirty dishes pilin' clear up to the rafters.'

The Saint watched Mildred's reactions to the speech and saw that she was delighted with the idea—though her eager expression wilted a little at the mention of dirty dishes.

'Well, Pat,' he said, 'I couldn't have thought of a better plan myself. If this poor misguided child honestly prefers us to the SS, she's welcome to come along. Maybe a little fresh country air will clear our heads and give us some good ideas for the next step.'

Mildred was ecstatic.

'You really don't mind?' she said excitedly. 'You'll let me come?'

Simon nodded.

'And I think the sooner we get on our way the better. It's just possible those guardians of yours recognized my face and could trace us here.'

She gave him a puzzled look.

'Why should they recognize your face?'

Her ignorance offended Kelly's pride of friendship.

'Good heavens, girl! Haven't ye heard of the Saint? Simon Templar—the Saint?'

He seemed to think that if he spoke the name to her loud enough she would be bound to recognize it. But she looked at him blankly.

'Saint?' she said.

'Never mind,' said Simon. 'Remember, she's been cooped up in a convent for over twenty years.'

There was a ray of dawn on Mildred's face.

'You mean you're famous,' she said. 'And I didn't even know it. I'm so sorry.'

'Didn't they give ye any newspapers or anything in that place?' Kelly inquired, as Simon asked their waiter for the bill.

'They were very careful about what I saw,' Mildred explained. 'No newspapers or magazines. I was brought up to think of my father as a great hero who tried to save the West from Bolshevism, and I was told that even though he had lost the war there were still millions and millions of people who believed in his cause and were only waiting for something to give them the courage to stand up and be counted. Then one day I came across something in one of the convent's books that showed me some of the other side of the story. I guess with all the books they let me read they were bound not to screen them all quite carefully enough. So when I realized what the rest of the world seemed to think of my father I was shocked.'

'Made ye see the light, did it?' Kelly said.

'Well, naturally I didn't just turn right around and deny everything I'd been taught since I was born—but I had enough doubts to want to find out both sides of the story before I let anybody use me to lead a big political movement. That's why I ran away.'

Simon stood up, putting money on the table.

'A wise decision,' he said. 'Now I think you'd be safer coming up to my room while Pat and I pack than staying down here by yourself.'

'If ye don't mind,' said Kelly. 'I'll have a final spot o' gargle for me nerves, and then I'll be off to get me things.'

Mildred went with Simon out to the lobby as Pat waved down the waiter. Most hotel guests who were going out were out by now, and the receptionist, a blonde woman, was intent on her record books. A dowdy man in a rumpled suit was reading a newspaper nearby. Then a porter came through the main entrance from the street carrying a pair of expensive-looking leather bags. Behind him walked a tall thin gentleman of about fifty-five, with a strangely egg-shaped head, long grey hair falling thick on the back of his neck, and bulging brown eyes. He was obviously in a hurry, and with those enormous compelling eyes fixed on the receptionist towards whom he was heading he did not notice the Saint and Mildred, who by then had just reached the elevator at one side of the lobby.

Simon would have thought nothing about the newcomer if it had not been for Mildred's reaction. In a fraction of a second all the colour drained from her face and she gasped audibly.

'I'll be back in a minute,' she whispered, averting her head. 'Ladies' room.'

And she disappeared into a public corridor next to the elevator.

Naturally the Saint's former lack of interest in the stranger immediately increased by one hundred per cent, and he sauntered back into the vicinity of the reception desk and pretended to study the contents of a magazine rack. The rumpled man with the newspaper was likewise affected by the guest's arrival. He got to his feet, put down his paper, and hovered expectantly like a suppliant waiting his moment to petition the passing emperor.

'Good evening, sir,' said the blonde receptionist pleasantly. 'Do you have a reservation?'

The protuberant eyes fixed her scornfully.

'I take it you do not recognize me?'

The woman, since she clearly did not recognize him, was a little flustered.

'No, sir. I'm afraid not. I . . .'

'It doesn't matter,' he grumbled. 'My name is Drew, and I have a reservation.'

She found his card quickly.

'Mr. Eugene Drew?' she said.

'That's correct.'

She pushed the register towards him and he scrawled a signature.

'I've read about you, Mr. Drew,' she said. 'In the papers. Consolidated Steel, and the coal mines, and . . .'

Her belated recognition of his importance failed to mollify him.

'It doesn't matter,' he said abruptly. 'Have you held the suite I requested?'

'Of course, sir. The porter will take you up.'

As Drew walked from the desk the man who had been waiting came up to him.

'Mr. Drew, sir,' he said in a low voice, with an ingratiating smirk, 'Me name is Blaney, correspondent for the *London Echo*.'

'Wonderful,' Drew remarked, with superciliousness that would have shrivelled an apple on the spot. 'Now if you'll pardon me...'

'Just a word,' wheedled Blaney, 'on the reasons for yer visit.'

'No comment.'

'Is there any truth in this talk ye're interested in buyin' into the Hardacre Group?'

'Get out of my way.'

Drew stepped around the reporter, who moved along with him crab-style.

'There's rumours, sir,' the reporter said in a more intense but less audible tone, 'that serious troubles in yer family have...'

Drew stopped and turned to face the speaker.

'I shall not forget your name, Blaney, and if you address one more question to me I shall contact Lord Abbeyvale, the proprietor of your paper, and request that he dismiss you immediately. I assure you he will respect my wishes.'

The reporter, beaten, backed away with cringing nods.

'Thank yer, sir. Thank yer very kindly in any case.'

As Blaney made his exit, Simon returned to the corridor down which Mildred had disappeared. Before he had gone more than a few steps, however, he heard Drew's name called breathlessly in the lobby he had just left. A glance over his shoulder told him that his alleged SS acquaintances from the trout stream had just come into the hotel—in dry clothes and unmuddied shoes—and were hurrying towards the elevator. They passed from his field of view, but he could hear the first exchange of words.

'Why are you alone?' Drew demanded.

'We thought we had her,' said one of the men, 'but some bloke interfered. We have a strong clue, though, and we'll soon pick up her trail, I'm sure.'

'Let's not broadcast it to the whole world, shall we?' Drew said in a sharp, hushed voice. 'Come to my room.'

There was a swoosh as the elevator doors closed behind them, and Simon was left with time for a few moments of silent meditation before Mildred rejoined him.

First, the SS man's speech had betrayed more influences of Liverpool than of Berchtesgaden. He had no German accent at all. That came as no surprise to the Saint, who by now had about as much confidence in Mildred's veracity as he did in the Flat Earth theory. The next obvious question was, then, what exactly was her relation to Eugene Drew?

Simon's speculations on that were delayed by the cautious arrival of Mildred herself.

'He's gone,' Simon said.

'Who?' she asked, wide-eyed.

'The man you were running away from.'

'I wasn't running away. I told you where I was going.'

The Saint pushed the elevator button.

'Your friends are here,' he said casually.

'What friends?'

'Your SS friends.'

She looked completely shattered, and all but pulled at the parting elevator doors to get inside, glancing fearfully over her shoulder.

'Where? Did they see you?'

'No,' Simon said. 'Nothing to worry about.'

He told the elevator operator his floor and discouraged Mildred from any more talking with a warning shake of his head. As soon as they were in his room she wanted to know everything.

'They came in and went straight for that fellow I thought you were avoiding,' said Simon, opening a suitcase on the bed and beginning to pack immediately, as Mildred paced up and down the Donegal carpeting.

'How could they have followed us here?' she asked, biting the edge of one of her pink-painted fingernails.

'I don't think they did. They seemed to have an appointment with the gentleman you weren't running away from—Eugene Drew.'

She showed no reaction at the name.

'You wouldn't have heard of him, of course,' Simon continued, 'considering the sheltered life you've led. But he's one of the biggest industrialists in Northern Ireland.

Mildred stopped pacing, and sucked in her lower lip.

'Maybe he's one of them,' she theorized suddenly. 'I heard them mention a man called Kleinschmidt, who changed his name and was some kind of Nazi agent here even before the war. He's probably scheduled to take over all of Ireland when they make their move.'

The Saint looked at her with a kind of ambiguous admiration.

'Fantastic,' he said. 'In a single day you've changed my whole picture of the history of our times.'

The phone rang, and Simon answered. It was Pat Kelly.

'I'm back in me own little room,' he said, 'and sober as a judge, in case ye're wonderin'. Shall we meet in the lobby in twenty minutes?'

'Fine,' said Simon. 'I'm just about ready now.'

He was travelling light, and he had not even removed most of his clothes—the ones for fishing and country wear—from the suitcase during his short stay at the hotel. So he had only to pack his toilet kit, and then he was ready to call for the porter.

'I think we'll send you down the stair well,' he said to Mildred. 'Your guardians wouldn't be likely to use it, and I'll meet you . . .'

There was a knock at the door. Mildred froze and her eyes grew wide.

'It's them,' she whispered.

'Clairvoyant too?' asked the Saint.

Mildred looked like a frightened rabbit.

'Who else could it be?'

'Maybe I've just won the sweepstakes,' the Saint suggested. 'But in case you're right, get in the wardrobe.'

She obeyed, and Simon hurried into the bathroom as the knocking continued. He took the bath brush from its rack and laid it on the edge of the washbasin so that the brush was under the tap. He put an empty plastic soap dish on the brush and turned on the tap just enough to produce a fast drip. Within a short time the soap dish would fill enough with water to unbalance the brush and make it fall into the basin. The whole operation took only a few moments.

Simon closed the bathroom door, making sure the key was in the outside. Then he pushed the door of the wardrobe firmly shut and went to answer the knocking. While he was prepared for anything, the Saint was nevertheless a little surprised to see Mildred's SS guardians standing there. He had considered the bath brush ticket a probable waste of energy.

But he did not show his surprise any more than he betrayed any concern over the pistol in the fat man's hand. His face was as serene as his afternoon had been before they and Mildred had interrupted it.

'Looking for the clown auditions?' he asked obligingly. 'The circus manager's room is next door.'

'Never mind,' said the man with the gun, displaying a notable lack of a sense of humour. 'Stand back.'

Simon obeyed, being sure that his calm retreat took him towards the closed bathroom door.

'Did you enjoy your swim?' he inquired.

'Where is she?' demanded the thin one.

'Who?' asked Simon.

'The girl.'

'Gone about her father's business, I suppose.'

'Mister,' said the fat one, 'you're getting in our way. I dislike violence, but if I have to I'll rub you out like a chalk mark.'

At that point the brush clattered into the washbasin, and Simon made an exaggerated move to put himself between the men and the bathroom door. The one with the gun stepped forward, then gestured for the thin one to investigate. There was a brief moment when the thin one was just inside the bathroom, and the fat one was off his guard, turning to peer over his companion's shoulder. That was the moment the Saint chose to use his foot, for the second time that day, on the posterior of the plumper of the pair, who was propelled forward through the doorway, striking his partner with something like the effect of a billiard on a ping pong ball. The thin man caromed into the shower stall, while the fat one carried enough momentum to send him stumbling to another corner of the little room. Simon quickly closed and locked the door, and almost before the captives had had time to start shouting and thumping he had opened the wardrobe and let Mildred out.

'Our friends have a great affinity for water,' he said, picking up the telephone and dialling Kelly's room.

'Oh, you're wonderful!' said Mildred. She stationed herself at the door for a quick getaway. 'How did you do it?'

'Pat,' Simon said, when his friend answered. 'I'm afraid the turnover in this hotel is a little fast for us. We'll have to hurry along and meet you at your house.'

Before the startled Irishman could reply, Simon hung up, lifted one of his suitcases in either hand, and followed

Mildred out into the corridor towards the elevator.

'What if ... Kleinschmidt is down in the lobby?' she asked.

'Kleinschmidt?' said Simon. 'Oh—the one who's taking over Ireland after the uprising. Well, I think I could handle him. If you prefer using the fire escape, go right ahead.'

She chose to come with him in the elevator.

'Here, now, sir,' the aged operator said, hurrying to take the suitcases. 'Couldn't ye get a boy for helpin' with those?'

'We were in a hurry,' the Saint answered. 'Some people were anxious to see us, but we weren't so anxious to see them.'

'Ah, and that's understandable enough,' said the operator with a wink, casting an appreciative eye over Mildred's shape and virgin ring finger. 'We'll have someone get those bags out front for ye now in a jiffy.'

Simon tipped him and walked with Mildred to the desk, where he paid his bill and asked for his car to be brought around to the main entrance.

'I heard a lot of banging on my floor,' he said to the clerk. 'Like somebody trying to break a door down.'

'I'll see to that, sir,' the clerk said, and rang for a porter.

'Oh, Mr. Templar,' Mildred said admiringly as they went out to the street, 'how did you ever lock up both those men?'

'It's no more miraculous than the fact that they knew where we were.' He looked at her closely. 'Is it?'

'I ... guess not. They're ... diabolical. They've got agents everywhere. And maybe they did recognize your face this afternoon, and found out where you were staying.'

The doorman stood by Simon's car at the curb.

'It's possible,' Simon said as he helped Mildred in. 'But I'm sure there's a simpler explanation. When we've had a chance to catch our breath, I want you to tell me the truth about it. If that won't be too frightful an effort.'

FOUR

As the Saint drove west through Dublin along the Liffey, he had the unmistakable feeling that his request for truth had put a damper on Mildred's ordinary talkativeness. She did not say anything, indeed, for more than twenty minutes. That fact was not totally without its charm, so Simon did not try to change the situation until they were driving through the dark countryside towards Leixlip and Kilcock.

'Now,' he said, 'how about telling me your real story.'

Mildred performed a flouncing jerk and twisted around so that she was facing her own side of the car. A moment later Simon heard whimpering sounds.

'I realize the thought of being honest must be terribly painful for you,' said the Saint, 'but try to bear up.'

There were snuffling noises, and then Mildred suddenly turned and looked through the back window.

'I think they're following us,' she said in an urgent voice.

'You're changing the subject.'

'No,' she insisted, wiping her eyes excitedly as she went on looking. 'I didn't mention it before, but I thought they picked us up just after we left the hotel. They must have got out of your room faster than we thought.'

'The Keystone Stormtroops?' said Simon. 'It doesn't seem very likely.'

'They're probably just staying back there waiting till we stop someplace where they can get me.'

In the rear view mirror Simon could see two pairs of headlights several hundred feet behind. He slowed his own car as a test of the others' reactions, and they began closing the distance at a normal rate.

'If they were following us,' he said, 'they probably wouldn't catch up like that.'

He increased the pressure of his foot on the accelerator.

'I can't help it,' said Mildred. 'I still think I saw them.'

'And I still think you're looking for ways to avoid talking about yourself, Miss Hitler.' He glanced at her. 'Or is it Anastasia? Bridey Murphy?'

Mildred gave a sigh, let her shoulders slump for a moment, and then sat up straighter and looked at him.

'I think you know who I am,' she said.

'I'm touched by your confidence.'

Mildred's voice had lost some of its little-girl quality.

'You saw me react when my father walked into the lobby at the hotel.'

'SS Führer Kleinschmidt is your father?'

'Eugene Drew is my father,' she replied patiently. 'And I think you've known all along.'

The Saint nodded.

'You seemed a little young to be Hitler's daughter—though there was a family resemblance.'

'Thanks.'

They were driving through Leixlip, and Mildred pointed to a pub on a corner just ahead.

'Oh, let's stop in there a minute! I feel like a beastly mess after all that snivelling—and I could use a shot of something.'

Simon slowed the car.

'I thought you were so worried about those goons you claim are following us.'

She looked back.

'Maybe I was wrong—and we've got to stop sometime. Anyway, what can they do in the middle of town? Drag me kicking and screaming out of the local?' She gave him a stern look, like a child threatening its parent. 'And if you won't stop here I'll never tell you *why* they're after me—and all the other juicy tidbits.'

Simon turned off the main street and pulled up across from the pub.

'All right, Mildred, or whatever your name is at the moment...'

'It *is* Mildred,' she interrupted.

Simon came around and opened her door.

'I guess we should celebrate your dropping old Adolf from your family tree,' he said.

'Righto! And where are we going from here?'

'To Kelly's place, of course, unless you've changed your mind.'

They crossed the quiet street, and Simon failed to see any sign of a lurking Mercedes in any direction.

'I mean where is Kelly's place?' Mildred asked.

'Somewhere east of Athlone, in the middle of nowhere. Why?'

'Well, naturally I'm curious.'

Simon was sure that his own curiosity at least equalled hers, and by now it involved much more than the simple questions of why she was so anxious to avoid her father, and why a certain pair of rather bumbling bloodhounds were so anxious to have her not avoid them. Two or three obvious explanations were at the top of his consciousness, but something told him that where Mildred was involved the obvious could never be automatically taken on trust.

He was content with the way things were going, though, and saw no reason to push the natural unfolding of events. The peace of his holiday was probably irretrievably lost, but peace had been replaced by the fascination of a Chinese magician's puzzle, in which illusion and reality were intriguingly mixed. Simon hoped, as a matter of fact, that the sleight-of-hand would not be entirely unmasked too soon. To be involved as he was gave the thrill of baiting a trout with a little brightly coloured imitation of life on the rippled surface of a stream.

It required patience, but a man of Simon Templar's relaxed confidence could always command a supply of that virtue.

The pub was dim, smoky, and redolent of stout and the honest sweat of hiking from home to the tap. A dozen and a half of what appeared to be neighbourhood regulars were enjoying the hospitality.

'Find us a table, will you, dear?' asked Mildred. 'I've got to go and repair the damage.' She indicated her face. 'And make mine a Guinness.'

Simon found a table in a corner, and the volume of talk, which had briefly diminished because of the arrival of a pair of strangers, soon returned to its original level. The barman took the Saint's order, brought it, in his own leisurely time, and several minutes later Mildred had still not returned. Finally, the Saint, aware of the insatiable addiction of some women for ritualistic applications of face paint, and secure in the knowledge that his car key was in his pocket, sat back with a sigh and began to drink alone.

When his share of the foamy dark liquid was half consumed, Mildred came back, looking cheerful and uncontrite.

'Now,' she said brightly, 'what would you like to know?'

She slipped into the chair beside him, propped her elbows on the table, and drank deeply from her glass, rolling her eyes to look at him as he answered.

'Let me see how much more you need to tell me. You're Eugene Drew's daughter. You obviously don't want to see Eugene Drew, but it seems that your father would like to see you. It seems, in fact, that he would like so much to see you that he has hired a couple of private investigators to find and catch you. Right so far?'

She nodded vigorously, her lips on the rim of her glass.

'Now, unless insanity runs in your family—which is a possibility I haven't by any means completely discounted—the most likely explanation is that you have run away from home and your poor distraught father is exerting every effort to bring you back into the fold. Just why you left home is another question. Maybe you did something naughty, like smother your little brothers and sisters, or hock your mama's diamond tiara, and you figure that any slaughtering that's done when you get back home will involve you instead of a fatted calf.'

She giggled.

'You've got it right up to the end. But my feelings are hurt.'

'Why?'

'Because you don't know why I ran away.'

Simon finished his stout.

'Should I?'

'Don't you read the newspapers?'

'When I can't find any really *good* fiction I sometimes sink to that.'

'Then why didn't you read about me?'

'I don't believe this escapade has been covered. I saw a reporter trying to worm something out of your father this evening. With no success, I might add.'

'That sounds like Dad. He's rotten about the papers. That's one reason why he was so absolutely furious when I ran away with Rick.'

'So there's another character in the cast,' said the Saint. 'Why haven't I had the pleasure of meeting this Rick, if you're running away with him.'

'That was last month. Rick is in America right now. It's Rick Fenton I'm talking about.'

Simon shook his head.

'Doesn't ring a bell.'

'Oh!' huffed Mildred, looking mortified. 'Rick Fenton, I mean. The *actor*.'

'Sorry,' Simon said. 'Has he played Hamlet?'

'He's a teeniebopper idol.'

'Sounds positively sacrilegious,' the Saint remarked. 'What is it?'

'You know ... all the teen-age girls scream and faint when they see him. He's twenty-two but he looks seventeen, and he's a really fantastic actor.'

'I'll bet he is,' said Simon.

'He was in *Beach Towel Tramp* and *Teen-Age Martian in a Girls' Dormitory*.'

'I missed both of those. You can tell what an alienated life I lead.'

'Anyway,' Mildred said with resignation, 'I ran away with him ... to get married. But they caught me, and it was in all the papers, with pictures and everything. There was one of Dad with his hat in front of his face. He almost *died*.'

Simon glanced at Mildred's glass, which was still two-thirds full.

'Why don't you drink up?' he suggested. 'We can talk in the car. It's still an hour and a half to Kelly's place.'

She obediently sipped a little of the stout.

'You don't want me to get drunk, do you?' she asked. 'I'm very susceptible.'

Simon sat back in his chair.

'You have thirty seconds,' he said, 'You used up most of your overtime in the powder room.'

Mildred tilted up her glass, gulped down several large swallows of Guinness, and went on talking, half out of breath.

'So this time I've run away to marry Rick,' she said. 'We're terribly in love, and my father is hopelessly stubborn and mean. He wouldn't want me to marry the . . . the King of Arabia.'

The Saint nodded.

'Probably not.'

'And so,' Mildred went on, 'Rick is stopping over at Shannon Airfield on his way from America to Paris on a personal appearance tour, and I'm going to join him.' She drained her glass. 'And rats to Big Daddy.'

'When are you meeting Rick?' Simon asked.

Mildred opened her mouth to speak, then closed it, and shook her head. She gave him a sly smile and wagged her finger.

'Oh, you won't get me to tell you that,' she said. 'What if I can't really trust you? That's all my father would need to know—when Rick was coming. Rick is smart. His publicity agent gave a false story to the papers, so as far as anybody knows, Rick isn't coming anywhere near Ireland.'

'Brilliant,' said Simon. 'Absolutely brilliant. And if you don't trust me, how do you know I won't turn you over to your father in return for a nice fat reward.'

She stared at him shocked, and clutched his arm as he stood up.

'Mr. Templar, you wouldn't! I thought I had to tell you, and I'd never believe you were the kind of person who . . .'

'Who'd stand in the way of true love? No, I suppose I'm not—not for the few paltry pounds I could squeeze out of a Scrooge like your father.'

'You're wonderful!'

She flung her arms around him, to the amusement of the other patrons of the public house, who unanimously became silent and grinned. It was probably the first time in the history of the establishment that there had been a total absence of talk during business hours for a period of four and a half seconds.

Simon left an overpayment on the table and steered Mildred out to the street, which was as empty as it had been when they first arrived. A few minutes later they were heading west out of town through the rolling moonlit countryside. Then Simon slowed the car a little.

Mildred shot him a worried look.

'You're not ... taking me back, are you?'

He shook his head, looking into the rear view mirror.

'What is it?' she asked.

She turned to peer through the car's back window as Simon put down the accelerator again.

'I think,' he said, 'to use the immemorial words of immemorial suckers, that this time we *are* being followed.'

FIVE

MILDRED began to show preliminary signs of hysteria.

'Oh, no! It's them! I know it is! I told you they were on to us before!'

'Maybe,' said Simon coolly. 'In any case, if you don't want to be embraced rather forcibly into the bosom of your family, you'd better get a map and flashlight out of the glove compartment. How's your navigation—or do you operate on intuition like your papa Adolf?'

She snorted as she scrambled for the map and flashlight.

'I was a Queen's Guide at school. I could navigate my way to the Christmas Islands just by watching which side of the fishes the moss grows on.'

She unfolded the detailed map of Ireland and turned the beam of light on it. The Saint had sped up along a straight stretch of road, and the other car was keeping pace about two hundred yards behind.

'You know where we are,' he said. 'See if you can find a place where we can turn off and lose them—and end up somewhere except in a peat bog.'

Mildred bent close to the map and studied it. The short-lived directness of the highway degenerated into a series of snaky curves through a wooded section marked by rocky hillocks.

'There!' cried Mildred suddenly. 'Up by that stone marker.'

'The Saint jammed down the brake pedal and swerved into the side lane. It was no more than a pair of wagon ruts made semi-respectable by an old topping of gravel. The way abounded with holes and humps, and Simon—driving without lights—was forced to slow to fifteen miles an hour in order to hold the car on its higher leaps to anything below treetop level.

Luckily, the other car had been too far behind around a curve to see what its prey had done. It swept by on the main road, its headlamps sending flickers of light through the woods.

'We lost them,' Mildred said jubilantly.

The Saint was less enthusiastic.

'For the moment. If they've got any brains at all they'll see in a minute they've lost us and then they'll come back. Are there any other side roads near here that might confuse them?'

'Only one I can make out, and it looks like a dead end.'

Simon stopped and turned off the engine. Then he listened closely to the receding sound of the car that had been pursuing them. Before it passed completely out of earshot, the noise of wailing tyres on distant curves came to an abrupt halt. The Saint's sensitive ears just barely made out the gunning of the engine and a couple of brief screeching spins of tyres on asphalt.

'I think they've caught on,' he said. 'They're turning around.'

He started his own car and continued down the horrendous trail, which was surely experiencing the passage of the first self-propelled vehicle in lifetime that must have dated back at least to Finn MacCool.

'Oh,' said Mildred in a low voice.

She was looking at the map, her face bouncing in the pool of light just above it.

'What?' said Simon.

'You know that dead end road I mentioned?'

'Yes.'

'We're on it.'

The Saint's commentary was internal and sustained.

'I see,' he said finally, with devastating quietness. 'Mildred Hitler, girl guide, has done it again.'

At that point, the tortured car gave a sudden lurch and stopped, slumped at an angle towards Mildred's side. Mildred's head bumped the glass in front of her with a lack of force which the Saint found faintly disappointing.

He turned off the ignition.

'Well,' he remarked, 'that's the second immobilized car you can chalk up to your record today.'

Mildred rubbed her head gingerly and looked even more gingerly at Simon.

'What happened?' she asked.

'Without checking on details, I should say that we have fallen into a hole.' He took a deep breath and opened the door. 'So ... let's start walking. Under different circumstances I might stand and fight, but at the moment I really can't think of anything worth fighting for.'

He walked around the front of the car and looked briefly at the damage. The wheel had slipped into a deeply eroded channel.

Mildred picked her way over the stones to join Simon.

'Can't you reverse out?' she asked.

'No. And I think the axle's bent anyway.' He looked at her. 'If your Papa Adolf's superman theories amounted to anything, you'd be able to lift up the whole mess and set it straight again.'

Mildred did not answer, and Simon set off down the road in front of the car with swinging strides. Mildred hobbled and stumbled behind him in her high heels.

'Wait!' she cried finally. 'I can't keep up.'

'Stay behind then. I'm afraid you've used up your allotment of my chivalry. If the wolves catch you, they won't bother chasing me.'

She let out a despairing wail and hurried after him up a moon-silvered hill, where the wagon track was thickly hedged with trees.

'Or maybe,' Simon mused happily as he trudged along, hands in his pockets, 'the little people will get you.'

'Little people?' Mildred whimpered, catching up a bit.

'Sure. Leprechauns. This is just the spot for them. You look a bit pixyish. They might take you for one of their own.'

'Damn!'

Mildred's exclamation had not been evoked by fear of Irish fairies. She balanced on one foot and held out her shoe for Simon to see. The stiletto heel had broken off.

'I can't walk like this,' she moaned.

'Let's see the other shoe,' said Simon.

She stood in her stocking feet and handed it to him. He grasped the remaining whole shoe firmly in both hands and snapped its heel off.

'There,' he said proudly, handing it to her. 'Now you're back on an even keel.'

She threw both shoes on the ground and vigorously recited a phrase which she most definitely had not learned either in a convent or as a Queen's Guide.

'I'd advise you to wear those,' the Saint said, starting up the hill again. 'They're better than nothing—and your faithful followers may discover this road at any minute.'

She clumped along beside him in the modified shoes, panting and clinging to his sleeve for occasional support. Simon looked up at the stars.

'Now is the time for fortitude and inner strength,' he philosophized. 'Keep the image of Rick firm in your mind. The course of true love never did run smooth.'

They went on for ten minutes, and then they saw the reddish glow of a fire through the trees at the base of the hill. Simon led the way and looked cautiously into the small clearing. Around a bonfire stood or sat five people, as yet oblivious to Simon's and Mildred's arrival. There were a man and woman of late middle years, and a pair of girls and a boy ranging from about twelve to eighteen. All of them were devoting their attention to a soot-blackened metal pot which steamed over the fire, suspended from a tripod. Nearby, a pair of horses grazed at the edge of a tiny brook. Like parts of a stage backdrop on the border of the circle of firelight stood two barrel-headed caravans—large painted wooden wagons like horizontal kegs on wheels—in which the family lived, and which it was the horses' duty to pull.

'Gypsies,' whispered Mildred.

'A tinker, I think,' Simon said. 'They've been travelling over Ireland like this since the beginning of time.'

The older man, who was seated in a folding canvas chair—undoubtedly a recent addition to the tinker's inventory of household goods—waved his hand towards the pot and said to the boy, 'What's it now?'

The boy pulled a large thermometer from the liquid.

'Sixty-three.'

The older man turned to the adolescent girls.

'Put it in.'

The two girls each picked up a small sack and dumped its contents into the mixture while the boy stirred with a long wooden stick.

'Is that ... potheen?' Mildred asked Simon in a hushed voice.

'It must be. The most potent stuff this side of hell-fire and brimstone. Let's go in quietly and peaceably, but not as if we're trying to sneak up. People who make illicit whiskey tend to shoot first and find out later whether their guests were revenue agents.'

As he and Mildred first appeared in the wavering, golden light the boy looked up from the pot and shouted, 'Hey!'

For a moment the whole tableau was absolutely motionless. Even the heavy-necked horses seemed to sense the drama of the moment and froze in position. Then, like a squad of American football players shifting into a defensive formation, the whole family moved. The three women stood between the newcomers and the bubbling cauldron as the men stepped forward, the elder first, the younger just behind. Simon and Mildred waited.

'They don't look friendly at all,' said Mildred out of the corner of her mouth.

'They're not,' the Saint said simply. 'Now's a good chance for you to use your greatest talent. Think of some lie to make them love us.'

Smiling pleasantly, he stepped forward towards the grim-visaged men.

'Good evening. Our car broke down on the lane. We saw your fire.'

The older man squinted at him for a long moment, chewing on a splinter of wood. A cap, which looked as if it might never have been removed since it was first put on years before, effectively de-emphasized his cranium and eyes, and brought into full prominence the mushroom effulgence of his scarlet nose.

'Main road is behind ye,' he said finally.

Mildred came to the rescue then. Her face suddenly went into contortions of pain, and she stood on one foot and clasped her arms around Simon's neck, letting him support her.

'I ... was hurt,' she gasped, 'when our car went in the ditch.'

She tried bravely to get her breath and stand straight again. Sympathetic glances were exchanged by various members of the tinker's party.

'What ye want, then?' the eldest woman asked.

'Somewhere to stay the night,' Simon answered.

'This is not a hotel, mister,' she said.

Simon went forward another step.

'We're nothing to do with the revenue, if that's what worries you,' he said.

The woman closed ranks in front of the pot.

'We're just fixin' ourselves a bit o' stew,' the eldest said. 'Shure and why would the revenue care about that one way or the other?'

'What are ye, then?' asked the younger man.

Mildred took over again, bursting excitedly into rapid speech.

'Please ... we're running away from my stepfather to get married! He's a terrible man. He's already wasted away my mother's fortune, and he wants what little I have left. If he catches us he'll ... We need your help—desperately!'

She broke off, sobbing violently.

'It's the truth, is it?' asked the older man.

'She's been under a terrible strain,' Simon replied, avoiding any direct commitment as to Mildred's veracity.

The lead man had begun shifting uncertainly from foot to foot.

'Hould on,' he said.

His entire group went into a huddle near the fire.

'We'll be glad to pay,' Simon called, thus probably cutting several minutes off the secret discussion.

'Well now, 'tis all agreed,' the man said, straightening up and turning. 'Ye can stay with pleasure, if ye don't mind the company of a tinker and his family.'

He held out his calloused hand and Simon shook it.

'Delighted. And thank you very much.'

'Me name is Muldoon,' the tinker said. 'And this is me wife. That's me boy Sean, and these are Tessa and Genevra.'

'I'm Rick Fenton,' Simon said, 'and this is Mildred Kleinschmidt.'

They went to the fire, where the boy, Sean, was stirring the pulpy liquid again. Mildred half closed her eyes and stepped back as some of the violently odoriferous steam drifted into her face.

'Delicious-looking stew,' the Saint said solemnly.

'It will be, when it's finished,' said Muldoon, winking.

He pulled out the thermometer, looked, and dropped it back again.

'How would ye like a little of the finished product?'

'Fine,' answered Simon politely. Then he added, with concealed relief, 'But I'm afraid we won't be staying that long.'

'Oh, we have a sample here from the last batch.'

While Muldoon fetched the sample, his wife was questioning Mildred with great concern about her injuries and feeling her ankle for broken bones.

'Ye poor little bit of a thing,' Mrs. Muldoon murmured, with a reproachful glance at Simon. 'Runnin' away to be wed, and not even a pair o' decent shoes for yer feet.'

Muldoon came around the fire with a large pickle jar. He unscrewed the cap.

'See what ye think of that.'

Simon braced himself, tilted up the jar, and swallowed as little as possible. The effect on his tongue and mouth combined various qualities of iodine, gasoline, and molten lava. He was damp-eyed and speechless for a moment. Finally he found that some small remnant of his vocal apparatus had miraculously escaped destruction.

'Delicious,' he said hoarsely, but with an expression no different from the one his face would have worn had he just been treated to a cup of Olympian ambrosia.

Muldoon beamed.

'Here, come on,' Sean said crossly. 'Me arm's dropping off.'

Muldoon went to take a turn at stirring the cauldron.

'Tessa,' he called, 'go and fetch our guests somethin' to eat.'

Simon unobtrusively separated some notes from the fold of money in his pocket and offered them to Muldoon.

'Here you are,' he said, 'and many thanks.'

'Aw, it's too much,' protested Muldoon, tucking the money into his shirt nevertheless. 'Now why don't you and yer bride let me wife show ye yer quarters?'

Sean, who had walked off towards the horses and back again, aggrievedly rubbing his overworked stirring arm, suddenly stiffened and cried out.

'Hey, Dad!'

There at the edge of the clearing, their faces menacing in the dancing light, stood Mildred's hunters.

SIX

Simon's response was so prompt and inspirational that not even two seconds passed between Sean's cry and his own.

'Revenue men!' he yelled.

'The devil and it is!' roared Muldoon in outraged agreement.

He snatched his stirring stick out of the pot of potheen and charged across the clearing. His son charged too, grabbing up a makeshift cudgel from the heap of spare wood by the fire.

Simon's only worry was that the private detectives might have guns, but if they did they had no time to use them. Muldoon and Sean sailed in with sticks flying, and Mrs. Muldoon and her daughters armed themselves with cooking pots from a chest beside the nearest wagon and ran to join the fray.

Mildred, who had let out a little shriek as the battle commenced, stood as if petrified, her hand to her mouth. Simon, seeing that the beleaguered detectives were getting a sound enough drubbing without any help from him, ran to prod her into motion.

'It's time we were on the move again,' he said, towing her into the woods in a direction opposite the one from which they had arrived at the tinker's camp. 'Didn't a train pass over this way?'

'I don't remember,' panted Mildred.

'Not very observant for a Queen's Guide.'

They were out of range of the firelight, hurrying downhill, and Simon recognized the voice of one of the detectives above the mêlée.

'There! They ran over there!'

'I think your friends are after us,' Simon said. 'And the tinker's probably wondering what kind of revenue men those are, leaving behind a big pot of potheen to chase us.'

Mildred had reached the limit of her strength by the time they emerged from the woods and stood on the level surface of a railway embankment. The track came around a curve on their left and continued through a cut in the low hill to their right.

'I can't go on,' Mildred gasped. 'Let's just give up. Let them catch me.'

'After all this trouble?' said the Saint. 'Not on your life. I don't like losing even ridiculous games like this.'

He held her hand, leading her along the tracks to the comparative shelter of the cut, where an irregular rocky face of earth rose up almost straight on either side.

'At least we're not out in open moonlight here,' he said.

'What if a train comes along?'

'Then we'll be squashed.' He met her shocked expression with a shrug. 'It happens all the time to ants and caterpillars.'

Mildred held a finger to her lips.

'Listen,' she whispered. 'I think they're here.'

Simon heard the voices of two men in the woods not far away. Apparently the tinker and his tribe had been content to chase the detectives out of their camp, and then probably —confused as to whether they had been spotted by revenue agents or not—they would pack up and move on as soon as possible.

As Mildred and the Saint faced the track, their backs to

the face of the cut, the detectives were searching along the edge of the forest to their left.

'Let's move away from them,' Simon whispered. 'Here—through the cut.'

He and Mildred, keeping their bodies inconspicuously flattened against the low cliff, edged along the side of the track. The detectives' voices sounded louder. They had come out of the woods.

'Oh, no,' moaned Mildred.

'What?' Simon asked.

'I think I hear a train.'

'Yes. Exactly what I hoped!'

'Hoped? You said we'd be squashed!'

'Not if we're clever, agile ... and lucky.'

He was quiet as one of the detectives called to the other.

'I think they're hiding here somewhere. We'd have heard them running.'

'Right!' replied the other. 'You go on towards the cut. I'll check this way. Wish we could just shoot the bloody pair of them and have done with it. I'm fed up, even for a hundred thousand quid.'

'I'll *shut* you up, Finch, if you keep flapping your lip like that.'

Simon looked at Mildred with slightly raised eyebrows.

'A hundred thousand?' he whispered. 'Your father must love you very much.'

'He's despicable. And ... and I don't even know what anybody's talking about.'

Simon mused aloud as he continued moving towards the other end of the cut.

'This case gets more interesting every minute.'

'And that train's getting closer every second,' said Mildred.

What had shortly before been a distant rumble beyond the curve to their left was now such a growing noise that it was no longer necessary to whisper.

'We'd better hurry,' the Saint said.

Just at that moment, the fat man, nosing along near the rails outside the cut, spotted them and shouted the news to his partner. But just as he started to run in after them the sound of the train mounted towards a roar and the blazing, unsteady light of the engine swept around the curve a quarter of a mile away. The detective back-tracked and ran up the hill along the edge of the cut, peering down to keep his eye on the Saint and Mildred.

'This way,' said Simon.

No longer making any effort to hide what he was doing, he grabbed Mildred's hand and ran with her through the cut as the brilliant headlight of the train caught them in its beam. The fat detective saw that they were heading across the tracks to the opposite side of the cut. He screamed to the thin one, who was still on the ground which was level with the tracks.

'Get across there! They're going up the other side!'

The thin one made a dash towards the tracks, then leaped back as he calculated that the engine would arrive abreast of his present location just as he arrived in front of the engine. The engine driver, seeing people running along the rails, applied brakes, but with no chance of even slowing appreciably before he was well past the cut.

The Saint had no intention of ending his shining career in so messy or pointless a way as being flattened by an Irish goods train while helping a fluff-brained girl run away from her father—or whatever it was she was really doing. He made certain that they got to the end of the cut ahead of the train, and then as the engine roared past, blaring infuriated warnings on its whistle, he dragged her up the lip of the cut opposite the fat detective, who could only watch, shouting and waving his arms.

He probably could scarcely even hear his own words, which were hopelessly swallowed in the click-clacking thunder of the passing grain wagons. The Saint waved at him pleasantly, bowed and tapped a greeting from his forehead. Then he took Mildred's hand.

'Get ready to jump,' he said.

She stared at him, appalled.

'*Jump?*'

'Of course. This couldn't have been handier if we'd had it planned by a travel agent.'

It was only three feet down to the moving tops of the cars and the train had just reached its minimum of speed brought on by the brakes.

'We'll stand back a little bit, then take a running jump,' Simon said. 'There'll be nothing to it—as long as you don't jump short and fall down between the train and the wall.'

'I won't do it!' cried Mildred.

'Yes, you will. Remember dear Rick. Get ready now. Last grain wagon.'

The detectives, who were now together on the other side of the cut, sensed the Saint's intention and were getting ready to jump in case he did. That was why he waited until the last grain wagon was passing—and the last half of that—until he grasped Mildred's hand more firmly than ever, ran forward, and leaped.

When they landed, the Saint, like a cat, kept his balance, and for an instant was able to see the frustrated faces of the detectives not eight feet from his. Then they were left helplessly behind, watching the red warning lights on the rear of the train, like mocking eyes, disappear towards the southwest.

Simon sat down and made himself comfortable on the roof of the wagon. Mildred was lying down on her stomach, but once she caught her breath and got over the first fear of perching on top of a swaying, incredibly jolting train which appeared in danger of toppling off its rails at any moment, she also sat up cautiously and looked around.

'We'll stay here at the top of the ladder,' said the Saint. 'Then if we see a tunnel coming up we can climb down and get on the flat-bed wagon behind.'

Mildred made a piteous groaning sound as she leaned slightly towards the edge of the roof and looked beyond the handrails of the ladder at the ground blurring by near the train. The engine had picked up full speed again now, and the wheels chattered almost lightly on the track.

'I wouldn't climb down that for anything,' she said.

Simon shrugged.

'Then you can just hope no tunnels come up.'

Mildred covered her head with both hands.

'And this wind is ruining my hair! Why did I ever let you get me into this mess?'

Even to a man as hardened as the Saint was to human ingratitude, and especially to feminine foibles, Mildred's last question was rather hard to take, and he considered tossing her off into the first soft-looking ditch. But that would have been like throwing away a key piece of the puzzle which was just beginning to take shape.

He looked at her elfin face in the moonlight as they sailed past forests and sleeping cottages and wondered what the final truth about it would be. He no longer believed a word of what she had told him about herself, her family, or her plans, but there was no way to wring the truth from a slippery liar, who would scoot from any man's grasp like a wriggling fish. He would have to play along with her until one among the dark hunches in his mind moved into the light.

Maybe she was an exceptionally large and pretty female leprechaun. The thought amused and pleased him, because in Celtic legend a leprechaun, when caught, reveals a hidden treasure.

SEVEN

THE final leg of the Saint's nocturnal odyssey with Mildred was prolonged but uncomplicated. At the town of Kildare they lay low on the roof of the wagon and no one saw them. From there the track turned briefly from southwest to west, and then bore northwest directly into the country between Lough Reagh and Lough Derg—two of the great Irish lakes—where Kelly lived. After less than twenty miles on the northwest course there was a stop at Tullamore, and after fifteen more miles they were at Athlone, on the lower end of Lough Reagh.

There, while the train was stopped, they climbed down the ladder of the grain van and strolled away so nonchalantly that not even the guard, busy with his oil can, gave them a second glance as they passed.

They made the rest of the trip by taxi—an old and sagging conveyance whose driver apparently picked up a few extra shillings on off days by hauling pigs to market in the back seat. The driver was even older and more sagging than his cab, and he begrudged his passengers every mile he carried them. He had two desirable traits, however: he spoke not a word, and he knew the countryside down to the last compost heap and culvert. Though his response to Simon's rather uncertain directions was an ambiguous grunt, he took off along the dark, twisting lanes of the rural landscape like a horse on its way back to the barn for supper. In an amazingly fast ten miles he deposited them at the gate of a white thatched cottage which stood alone in the midst of high hedges at the edge of some cleared fields. Simon recognized Kelly's car and knew they had come to a resting place at last.

The taxi driver took the payment and generous tip, looked at the notes and coins as if they were a handful of dead cockroaches, and rattled away towards town.

'What a lovely place,' Mildred said. 'I didn't know your friend was a farmer.'

'In a small way,' Simon answered.

He opened the gate and let Mildred go ahead.

'Pat Kelly used to be the kind of man who was never happy spending more than six months in any one place, but his wife blew the whistle on him after he almost got his head hacked off in the Congo, and now he seems to be pretty content.'

The subject of their discussion opened his front door, and a wedge of light fell on Simon and Mildred.

'So here ye are at last!' bellowed Kelly.

'At last,' Mildred sighed, dragging her way across the threshold.

'And where's yer car and all?' Kelly asked. 'What happened at the hotel?'

The small living room of the cottage was made to seem even smaller by the amount of furniture and bric-à-brac crammed into it. Kelly's wife's interests were represented by china dolls, ornate clocks, and corner shelves laden with an indescribable assortment of glass and gold-leafed souvenirs—most of them bearing the word 'souvenir' at some prominent point on their surface.

Kelly's mementoes were along martial or exotic lines: an antique sword, African spears, shrunken heads, and primitive shields and masks. Perhaps as a countermeasure against that heathen paraphernalia, there were also on the walls violently hued lithographs of the Sacred Heart and the Virgin Mary.

'It's a long story,' Mildred said.

She collapsed into an overstuffed chair with such a show of exhaustion that Kelly immediately looked shamefaced and apologetic.

'Shure, and it's a poor way I'm behavin' to welcome ye after yer journey with a lot of questions. Sit down, Simon, and I'll fetch some rejuvenatin' potions from the supply I brought out with me from Dublin.'

Simon's stamina was remarkable, but he had nothing against a little relaxation at that point. It was after one o'clock—time enough to call it a day. He sank into one of the chairs opposite Mildred, stretched, and let his muscles go comfortably limp. Kelly, who had gone out through a dining alcove to the kitchen, came back with several bottles grasped by their necks in one of his massive hands, and the glasses held in the other.

'We may go hungry, but never thirsty,' he said, 'and that's the important thing.' He set the bottles and glasses on a low table and began to pour. 'Did ye know that a man can go weeks without eatin' but all it takes is a few days without liquid, and...'

He snapped his fingers expressively. Then he turned to hand Mildred her filled glass and saw that she had fallen asleep. Her head had flopped to one side, and her mouth was half open. She looked about fourteen years old.

'The poor girl,' Kelly whispered, turning to the Saint with another glass. 'What have ye been doin' to her?'

Simon looked at her wind-blown hair, her smudged face, her dusty suit, her now shoeless feet and laddered stockings.

'You might ask what she's been doing to me.'

'What then, man? I'm on pins and needles. Have the Nazis taken over the west of Ireland? They can have the north and be welcome to it, but if they come here...'

'The Hitler's daughter routine is a thing of the past,' Simon said.

Then he paused, looking suspiciously at Mildred's child-like face.

'Before I tell you, is there a bed for her?'

'Shure. Me daughter's room. Let's put her there. And you can have what me wife is fond of callin' the guest room, only till now there's never been a guest near it. There's a lot of spare gear, but I think we can clear a path to the bed.'

Simon stood up and went to touch Mildred's shoulder.

She did not stir even when he spoke her name, so he scooped her into his arms and carried her as Kelly led the way to a little bedroom.

'Do ye think she might be a lot more comfortable without all them clothes on?' Kelly asked wistfully, when Simon had put her on the bed.

Simon steered his friend out of the door and into the hall.

'She might be,' he said, 'but it might have the opposite effect on you.'

'I don't suppose *you'd* care,' Kelly sulked, 'havin' been with her the better part of the night already.'

They were back in the living room, and Simon smiled as they sat down and picked up their glasses.

'If that was the better part of the night,' he said, 'I hate to think what the worst part has in store.'

'Well, have mercy and tell me what happened, would ye, before I split a blood vessel.'

Simon leaned forward and lowered his voice, jerking his head in the direction of Mildred's sleeping-room.

'There's just one thing,' he said. 'Do you have a telephone?'

Kelly nodded.

'Amazing as it may seem, we do. And light, as ye can see. But no runnin' water unless ye make it run by the strength of yer arm. Who'd ye want to call at this hour?'

'Nobody. But whatever you do, keep Mildred away from it.'

Kelly sat back impatiently and gulped at his drink.

'Now for heaven's sake why is that?'

'Because every time I shake those two men who're following her, they show up again faster than ...'

'The SS, you mean?' Kelly interrupted.

'Except they're not SS. According to her latest bulletin they're private detectives hired by her father to catch her and bring her home before she can get married to some American actor.'

'And who might her father be this time?'

'For the moment, Eugene Drew.'

Kelly looked enlightened, and amazed.

'The rich fella,' he said. 'It's like a holy miracle, but I just looked at tomorrow's paper I bought in the village and me eye fell on that story. A little squib in the back: rumoured that Eugene Drew's daughter has run away again—or somethin' to that effect.'

'Was that all it said?' the Saint asked.

'It was only a couple of lines.' Kelly's voice became alarmed. 'But Simon, you helpin' a runaway—and she here in me own house! It's a dangerous game to be playin' and for no good reason. And what's this about detectives findin' her, and her and the telephone and all? Shure and she's not callin' the very people she wants to get away from and tellin' them where she is! She may be crazy, but that's carryin' insanity to obnoxious extremes.'

The Saint's calmness was a marked contrast to Kelly's excitement.

'I wouldn't discount any possibility right now,' he said.

'They knew I had a room at the hotel when they shouldn't even have known my name. They caught up with us outside Dublin when they shouldn't have had the faintest idea which way we were going.'

'Maybe she's got one o' them homin' devices planted on her,' Kelly suggested. 'I saw a film last week where they put some pin in this man's lapel, and then they could know where he was no matter...'

Simon grinned and shook his head.

'There's no need to make it so complicated,' he said. 'Nothing has happened that can't be explained by a little behind-the-scenes use of the common telephone.'

Kelly jumped to his feet impatiently and poured himself a fresh shot of whiskey.

'There ye' are again—back to her and the telephone. If I've got a lunatic—or maybe two—under me roof, I'd at least like to know how she—or they—came to be here, so fill me in as directly as ye can.'

By the time Simon had given a strictly factual account of everything that had happened from the time he had left Kelly in the Gresham Grill until he and Mildred had arrived at Kelly's cottage door, it was late enough that he definitely preferred sleep to the Irishman's exotic speculations as to the truth behind the events.

'Let's sleep on it, Pat,' the Saint said, getting to his feet. 'The best thing you can do is see that Mildred doesn't use the phone or leave your house.'

'Ye talk as if ye won't be here,' said Kelly.

'Well, my car—or what's left of it—is sitting with a bent axle in the woods somewhere west of Lucan. If you don't mind, I'll borrow your car and drive back there to see about having it towed out and repaired. I'm afraid I'd never get much action if I just telephoned. They'd probably want my personal authorization to take it, and it's in a pretty obscure spot.'

'Ye're welcome to me car,' Kelly said, 'but we could all go if ye like.'

'I have a feeling you and Mildred will both be asleep, and I'd like to get an early start. Anyway, I'm afraid if we once let her out of the house we'll mysteriously find that her chums are on our trail again.'

'But Simon, me boy, we can't be holdin' her prisoner, and why should we? I mean, it isn't us that's runnin' away with her—and if me wife should come home unexpectedly and find her here, it'd be . . .'

'I'll back up your story,' said the Saint. 'And before I turn in I'll explain what I have in mind. If Mildred's story is on the level, she'll be glad to hole up here till it's time for her to meet her boy friend at the airport. She'd be a fool to show her face anywhere until the very last minute. Right?'

Kelly nodded his shaggy red head.

'Now,' Simon continued, 'if she's not telling the truth, and if she *is* the one keeping the hounds hot on her own trail, then the whole show must be for somebody else's benefit.'

Kelly was swaying uncertainly on his feet, frowning in the intensity of his effort to understand what Simon was saying. He had drunk the entire contents of at least one of the bottles.

'Benefit,' he mumbled vaguely. 'Whose benefit?'

'So far you and I are the only audience I know anything about,' the Saint replied.

'Ye mean it's all a big joke?'

'No. I think it's possibly a big show with a starring role written in for me. And since I'm one of the leading characters I just want to be sure there's going to be a happy ending.'

'Ye've lost me,' said Kelly.

'Well, ponder on it,' Simon said, 'and by morning I'm sure you'll have come up with some of the same possibilities I have.'

'It'll do me no earthly good to ponder at all,' Kelly said, showing the way to Simon's room. 'Me wife says I'm good for nothin' but fightin' and drinkin' and sometimes I'm inclined to believe her.'

'You may have a chance to prove she's right about the fighting if Mildred's detective friends show up tomorrow.'

Kelly grunted.

'Listen—even the postman can't find this place, let alone a couple of city yobbos like them. And if they do get here...'

He raised his fist expressively.

'That should discourage them,' Simon said. 'Hold down the fort, Pat, and if I'm gone when you get up I should be back by mid-afternoon.'

The next morning went according to the Saint's plans. He needed no alarm clock to guarantee that he would wake up by a certain hour. He told himself before he fell asleep that he wanted to be awake at nine, and when he opened his eyes to the sun his wrist watch told him that his mental timer had been accurate almost to the minute. A short while later he was on the road that ran through Mullingar to Kilcock, about sixty miles from Kelly's house. As he drove through the beautiful countryside, admiring the red and purple fuchsia against the whitewashed walls of cottages, he thought of the fishing he might be enjoying at this moment. Somehow or other he was going to extract a compensatory reward from this adventure, even if it took selling Mildred to an Arab slaver.

There were no more complications than might have been expected involved in having his car retrieved from the wilderness. He showed a towing truck from Kilcock the way, and the job was done in short order. The repair of the axle would take overnight, he was told, since parts would have to be obtained from Dublin. So he transferred his luggage from the boot of his damaged car to the boot of Kelly's, had a simple but decent lunch at a Kilcock hostelry, and drove back the same way he had come earlier.

It was after four when he stopped in front of Kelly's cottage. The vine-covered gate was standing open. The door of the cottage was open a few inches also. In the living room, several pieces of furniture were overturned, one of the wooden African masks was broken in half and a Zulu assegai was embedded in the sofa. There was no blood, at least, and there were no bullet holes.

On the nail in the wall where the primitive mask had hung was a note on white paper. Simon took it down and read it.

Saint:

We have your friend and Mildred Drew. Tell Eugene Drew that if he wants to see her alive he must give you a hundred thousand pounds which you must deliver to us tomorrow night at the crossing marked on the map below at nine o'clock. Come alone. Your friend won't be hurt if you co-operate, and neither will the girl. Otherwise we'll kill them.

EIGHT

EUGENE DREW turned from the floor lamp and looked at the Saint with his uncommonly large and protuberant eyes. Then he turned back, held the note in the direct light of the bulb, and read it again.

It was nine o'clock in the evening of the same day on which Simon had plucked the note down from a nail on the wall of Kelly's cottage. Arranging to see Drew had been momentarily difficult because the man was obsessed with the notion that nine-tenths of the newspaper reporters on earth were devoting themselves exclusively to scheming ways of invading his privacy. But Drew knew of Simon Templar by reputation, and there was also the note, as concrete evidence.

Still, the financier had made no secret of his mistrust when he admitted the Saint to his suite at the Gresham. He had stood there tall and slope-shouldered in a grey tweed suit much too heavy for the season, and with a total absence of cordiality or even politeness held out his hand.

'The note,' he had said.

Simon, with no greater display of warmth, had given it to him.

Now Drew, after the second reading, turned from the lamp and placed the paper on a table. He gave it a final glance and looked at the Saint, who had made himself comfortable in an armchair.

'You believe this note was left by the detectives I hired to find my daughter?' Drew asked.

'I'm reasonably sure of it. But it doesn't really matter, does it? The problem is the same, whoever the kidnapper is.'

Drew paused, made a grunting sound of assent, and paced towards the window.

'I'm paying Brine and Mullins—the detectives—a salary much higher than they would normally be paid, and I promised them a large bonus if they were successful. Why should they risk everything, including their freedom, for...'

He stopped, shook his head, clasped his hands behind him, and paced again.

'Maybe they don't have so much to risk,' Simon said. 'A private detective's pay wouldn't make a truck driver very envious. Maybe once you gave them a whiff of higher things they just couldn't resist the temptation to try for the jackpot. I assume your bonus didn't approach a hundred thousand pounds.'

'Of course not,' Drew snapped. 'After all, she's just a silly little child running off to try to ruin her life with some long-haired nincompoop of an actor. There was no reason why I should offer a queen's ransom to anybody just for tracing her. I offered more than I might have because when Brine and Mullins came to me and said they had a clue as to her whereabouts...'

'The detectives came to you?' Simon interrupted.

'Yes. When Mildred disappeared I began putting out quiet feelers immediately. Brine and Mullins got wind of what was happening and came and told me that they believed they could return my daughter within forty-eight hours—and without publicity. They asked a stiff price, but it seemed worth it.'

'Well,' said the Saint, 'if they were honest in the first place, it would seem they got carried away by the heat of the hunt and decided to go crooked. I'll have to admit we were leading them a merry chase there for a while.'

'And that's something else, Mr. Templar,' Drew said, glaring at him. 'Your summary of events on the telephone failed to explain just what you were doing with my daughter in the first place.'

'If you had been listening closely, you'd recall I said she insinuated herself into my good graces by telling lies. To be specific—that she was Hitler's daughter and that your detectives were SS men.'

Drew all but spat on the floor.

'That's preposterous!'

'Don't blame me for weak points in Mildred's upbringing. And just keep in mind that even though I was clever enough to surmise that she wasn't really Hitler's daughter, I had no way of knowing whose daughter she really was. By the time she confessed, we were a long way from Dublin.'

'Why didn't you call me immediately, as soon as you knew who she was?'

Drew's imperious tone irritated Simon, who sat quietly for a moment, the sapphire points of his eyes fixed penetratingly and coldly on the other man's face.

'Remember, Mr. Drew, I'm not one of your hired lackeys. Your daughter—probably accurately—made you sound like a selfish ogre. I saw no reason to stop her doing anything she pleased.'

Drew glowered for a moment longer, then turned angrily away. The Saint got to his feet.

'Now,' he said, 'are you going to pay up, or lose one of your tax deductions the hard way?'

Drew's face was now more apprehensive than angry.

'You don't think they'd ... actually kill her?'

'I'm afraid unsuccessful kidnappers are more dangerous than successful ones.'

'What guarantee do I have they'll return her even if I do pay the money?'

Simon shrugged.

'None. That's one reason why I consider kidnapping one of the more nauseating crimes in the human repertoire. But if you don't pay, the odds are something like fifty to one in favour of their killing Mildred. If you do, then naturally Brine and Mullins would rather look forward to enjoying their fifty thousand pounds apiece without a murder rap hanging over their heads. I'd advise you to pay.'

'Naturally,' Drew said, hardening his tone again. 'Naturally you would. The note conveniently specifies that you and only you may bring the money. Let's assume that you are not a part of this plot. That assumption may be erroneous, but for the sake of argument...'

Simon held up his hand and gave Drew a look of cold contempt.

'I was afraid you might make such nasty insinuations,' he said levelly. 'So, to demonstrate my sincerity, I'll simply remove myself from the whole situation and let you worry about it.'

He stepped towards the door. Drew moved after him quickly, his face showing sudden panic.

'No ... Wait. I ... I apologize.'

The Saint turned back, his expression only slightly softer, making it plain that he was not quite sure that the apology was adequate.

'What were you saying then?'

Drew opened his mouth, paused, and closed it again.

'Ah ... I'm not sure,' he said.

'I think I can read your mind,' said the Saint. 'You were going to ask what would prevent me from setting off for the crossroads with your money and going straight on to Brazil without even slowing down.'

'It's a natural thought,' Drew said, with a conspicuous lack of the truculence his voice had carried a few moments before.

'I suppose it is, for the kind of man who would do it,' Simon responded pleasantly. 'But I'm not that sort of man. And besides, they have an old friend of mine along with your daughter, and I wouldn't like to be responsible for his being hurt. Does that reassure you?'

'Yes.'

'Then you'll have the money by tomorrow night?'

Drew nodded.

'Yes. Where will I find you?'

'I'll be staying here tonight and for the day tomorrow. I'm getting tired of covering the road between Dublin and Lough Reagh. At four tomorrow afternoon I'll come to your suite here and pick up the cash. Then if everything goes well, Mildred and my friend will be free before midnight.'

'All right,' said Drew. 'I'll have to trust you.'

Simon paused at the door.

'Yes. You should. Don't try to follow me or have me followed. It may seem like a smart idea at first thought, but if Brine and Mullins suspected anything they might bolt before I could pay them—and possibly they'd do something drastic on their way out.'

'It'll be in your hands then,' Drew said.

For the first time he showed signs of letting his tenderer emotions get control of him. His huge eyes moistened and his mouth threatened to tremble.

'And ... tell Mildred,' he mumbled, 'that who she marries is her own business, if that's how it has to be. I won't stand in the way.

'I'll deliver the message. It seems like a wise one.'

The Saint looked at Drew more intently. His final request, towards which it might be said that all the earlier part of his conversation had been secretly building, would have to be phrased in such a way as to arouse no suspicions. To slip now would be like settling weight on a false footing just inches before reaching the top of a precipice.

'There's just one thing I'm curious about,' he said.

'What?' Drew asked.

'You're very concerned about who has captured your daughter, and all about my character. I'm sure you'll have me checked out thoroughly before I get my hands on that money tomorrow. The one thing you haven't thought to ask is whether or not the kidnappers have your daughter.'

Drew was obviously taken aback. He looked a bit like a schoolboy caught in a ridiculous arithmetical error.

'Well,' he said defensively, 'Brine and Mullins are far overdue in contacting me—which seems to confirm your story. My daughter, after all, *is* missing. And you're so anxious for me to trust in your honesty: it was you who was with her, and who told me you left her in the house where you found the note. I don't even understand what you mean, now . . .'

'I mean,' said Simon, 'that I have never seen your daughter—before yesterday. Do you have a picture of her?'

Drew seemed flabbergasted that the Saint would bring up such a crucial question of identification at that late moment.

'Yes,' he said. 'I brought this with me in case I had to ask the police to put out a public alarm.'

He went into the bedroom which adjoined the living

room of the suite and returned with a large photograph in his hand.

Simon took it and studied it. Then he smiled.

'Yes,' he said, taking a last satisfied look. 'That settles it.'

NINE

THE fat man called Brine sat in an old Austin-Healey at the crossing of two unpaved roads six miles from the village of Birr. It was two minutes before nine o'clock, and though the man must have been tired, since he could have had little sleep in the past twenty-four hours, he was as alert as a sentry on the border of enemy territory. His head jerked towards the direction of the slightest sound, and the Saint was sure that his hand must never be far from the ignition key, so that he could start the engine and be off at the first threat of danger.

So the Saint, who was crouched in the trees just behind Brine's car, had to be very quiet. The night was cloudy and thus exceptionally dark. That was one advantage. Another advantage was the mild but gusty wind which had come along with the cloudy weather. The noises it caused in the branches of trees and bushes would continually distract Brine and also tend to cover any sounds the Saint might make. Simon could have made do without those advantages, but their existence was convenient and seemed a good omen.

He crept forward like a stalking leopard into the road behind the car, carrying something in one hand which might have been even more alarming to Brine than a gun, had Brine been able to see it. It was a large can of white paint—a half gallon—with a strip of adhesive tape in the middle of both the top and the bottom.

When he had reached the rear of the car, Simon deftly

and silently hooked the handle of the paint can over one of the bumper guards. Then he pulled the strips of tape from the top and bottom. Under each piece of tape was a small hole, and white paint began to drip slowly but regularly on to the dark earth of the road.

With as little sound as he had made in coming, the Saint moved away from the car and melted into the murky forest like a passing shadow.

When he was a safe distance from Brine, he quickened his pace and quickly covered the two hundred yards of woods which separated the Austin-Healey from his own car. He had arrived in the area before Brine and parked in an obscure little lane which was visible from neither of the roads which formed the crossing marked on the crude map the kidnappers had left behind at Kelly's house. Now that his private mission with the can of paint was finished, it was a simple matter to start his engine, drive down to the crossroads, and arrive just on time for the meeting.

His car was facing Brine's when he drove up, and in the glare of his own lights he could see Brine gesturing for him to drive alongside. Apparently the erstwhile detective wanted to keep the road ahead clear for a fast getaway, and also had no intention of leaving the security of the driver's seat of his car.

Simon stopped so that his open window was less than two feet from Brine's. He was greeted with a dim view of Brine's pudgy face and the snout of a revolver.

'Got the money?' Brine asked nervously.

Simon, remaining in his car, picked up the attaché case which Drew had given him in the afternoon and handed it out through his window. Brine took it, dropped it on to the seat beside him, and kept his eye and gun on the Saint while his free hand fumbled with the latch. A few seconds later he held a handful of neatly stacked and banded notes alongside the gun, so that he could check their genuineness without dropping his guard. Then he put them back and inspected another handful. Obviously he was too nervous even to think of counting to see if the correct amount was there.

'This'd better be right,' he said. 'Any tricks and it's too bad.'

'It's good money,' the Saint said lightly. 'I wouldn't mind having some of it myself.'

Brine snorted.

'Give me your car key,' he said.

Simon took the key from the ignition and handed it to Brine, who promptly threw it off into the bushes.

'Now, Mr. Brine,' said the Saint with mild reproach, 'that isn't very original. But at least it shows you learn by example. How long did you have to dive in that river the other day before you found yours?'

'I haven't any time for talking, Templar?'

Brine started his car.

'What about Mildred and Kelly?' Simon asked.

'They'll be let loose somewhere near a telephone.' He grinned. 'Now if I were you I'd start hunting for that key.'

He pulled quickly away as Simon leaned down, tore a strip of tape from a niche under the dashboard, and inserted one of his spare keys into the ignition. The satisfaction he got from reaping the benefit of that bit of foresight was minor compared to his relief at seeing—when he flicked on his headlights and turned around—the spots of white paint clearly marking the route by which Brine's car had disappeared.

Simon set a rate of speed which he felt would keep Brine from widening the gap between them. The white spots turned on to a paved road which led south for several miles, and then turned off into the woods again. The spots were difficult to see on the rocky lane, but it did not really matter since once on that particular pathway it would have been impossible for a car to deviate to one side or the other without leaving behind a swathe of broken undergrowth.

A little further on the woods became more sparse, and the crude road wound up the side of a hill. At the top of the hill was one of those broken-down castles which do so much to enhance the beauty of Irish tourist brochures. Simon could see its single round tower black against the shredded clouds of the faintly luminous sky. With the lights of his car off, he drove to the edge of a grove which was within easy walking distance of the castle, but was far enough away that no one on top of the hill could have heard the sound of his engine or the careful opening and closing of the door.

The Saint stood for a minute looking up the slope at the crumbled heap of stone. If Brine or his partner had discovered the paint can on the bumper of the car, there could be trouble. The run up to the castle could be diversionary, and Simon would find that the white spots of paint led right off down the other side. That would mean, at the least, the loss of precious time. Worse, if Brine was on to the fact that he was being tailed, he could be lying in ambush somewhere among the broken walls above. But the Saint preferred to think that luck would stay with him. There was, after all, no logical reason for Brine to walk around and take a look at the rear of his car.

Simon chose the most direct path up the hill which offered a little cover in the form of scattered bushes and occasional low infrequent sections of an ancient stone wall. Probably stones from this wall as well as from the castle were a part of many a hearth in this neighbourhood: the peasantry of all countries tended to regard noble relics of the past as no more than convenient quarries for common use.

There were few trees on the upper part of the hill. In fact, now that Simon had covered two-thirds of the distance between his car and the castle there was only one gnarled trunk breaking the open ground. He ran silently to it, then stopped in its shadow and looked at the ruins, which were now less than a hundred and fifty feet away. There was no trace of light escaping the gloom of the walls, and he could hear nothing except the wind.

He took the pistol from the holster under his left arm and moved on more cautiously than ever, covering the last stretch so quickly and soundlessly that even if someone had glimpsed him he might have been taken for an illusion of the night.

He was at the outer wall of the castle now. It had never been a large establishment. As in the case of most such places of any real antiquity, the tower had been built first—and built to last despite the neighbouring lord's most vigorous efforts to knock it down. The peasants, in their search for chimney-stones, had not fared much better than the besiegers of former times. The tower still stood almost unscathed while the rest of the structure, built later with the knowledge that the old donjon could be used as the ultimate in defence, lay mostly fallen about it in heaps of rubble.

Simon went around one of the traces of wall and stopped suddenly, slipping behind a half-collapsed archway. There was Brine's car, no one in it, with the paint can still dripping from the bumper. From the tower just beyond the car there came an unmistakable mutter of voices. The Saint circled, keeping himself out of sight, until he could see light through an arrow-slit window. Then he moved in and had a cautious look.

What he saw in the room at the base of the tower would have been enough to cause at least a temporary paralysis of the breathing mechanism in a man of less prescience.

The chamber was lighted with a kerosene lantern. Kneeling on the floor was Brine, flicking open the catch of the attaché case which Simon had given him. Standing alongside was the thin detective, Mullins, showing large facial bruises which must have been a result of his encounter with the tinker and his family the night before. Brine bore some of the same marks.

This much of the lurid spectacle of thieves eagerly salivating as they prepared to inspect their spoils was not unusual or shocking. But there was a third person present: Mildred. She was standing next to Mullins, not with the air of a languishing princess, nor even with the tearfully grateful air of a formerly languishing princess who has just been ransomed. She was leaning forward with the look of a kitten about to be fed, and when Brine opened the case and grinned as he held up a double handful of fivers, she fell on to her knees beside him and hugged him around the neck.

'Oh, Dad!' she said. 'I can't believe we really did it!' She was mixing laughter with her words, and even the sullen thin man smiled until he stretched a split lip and winced as he covered his mouth with one hand.

'Well, now, Phyllis,' said Brine proudly, clapping the case shut again, 'you're proven you're a chip off the old block this time. Your mother would have been proud of you.'

Mullins shook his head nostalgically.

'True enough. What a pity Moll couldn't have been here to see this.'

Brine indulged in a moment of sadness, then shook off the feeling.

'Well, well,' he said. 'We must let the dead bury the dead. And that goes for Simon Templar, too.'

That remark produced a laugh from the two men, but ex-Mildred, now Phyllis, looked worried.

'You didn't hurt him?' she asked.

'Oh, no. But when Drew's daughter doesn't show up it'll be the Saint left holding the bag. Or holding nothing, I might say.'

He laughed again.

'What about his pal?' asked Mullins.

They all looked towards a closed door so thick and so heavy with metal bindings that even the centuries had not brought it down from its massive hinges.

'Leave him, of course,' shrugged Brine.

'We can't,' Phyllis said. 'He'd never get out, and he'd starve to death.'

Brine clicked his tongue.

'Ah, Phyllis, I must warn you that your mother Moll was undone by that same sort of sentimentality. She was the only woman ever arrested in the Seaman's Home while putting money *back* in a man's trousers when she found he had eight hungry children. Of course they never believed her story.' He looked around the chamber and concluded absently, 'I'm not sure I ever believed it myself.'

Mullins picked up a short length of rusted iron from the floor.

'This has a point on it,' he said. 'He can use it to work his way out.'

'All right, then,' Brine agreed impatiently, 'but hurry it up, would you?'

Mildred threw the bolt on the door.

'Now don't you try anything,' Brine called to the prisoner. 'I'll have a gun on you. Mullins is going to throw you a little something and you can chip your way out of there within a couple of days if you work hard at it.'

Simon did not get a look at Pat Kelly as Mildred opened the door a crack and Mullins tossed in the piece of metal, but he did hear his friend's voice, and it sounded gratifyingly robust and healthy.

'Ye bunch of cross-eyed orang-outangs! Let me out of here and I'll fix ye up with yer legs around yer necks so ye can see behind when ye walk!'

He went on in the same vein even after his words were muffled by the door slamming again. Simon, meanwhile, moved around the outside of the tower until he came to the entrance, which was a doorless irregular hole that led directly into the chamber he had watched through the window. He waited until Phyllis picked up the lantern and turned with Brine and Mullins to leave. Then he showed himself, lounging easily, automatic in hand, between them and freedom.

'Hello, friends,' he said, with a pleasant smile.

Phyllis was the first to recover her voice.

'Simon! How did you ... ever find me?'

'Your latest father left a trail,' he answered.

'What trail?' demanded Brine.

'*Father?*' cried Phyllis uncomprehendingly.

'Oh, Mildred Phyllis Hitler Drew Brine,' said the Saint with indulgent sadness, 'I'm afraid you've come to the bottom of the name barrel. Somewhere at the core of all those lies there had to be a truth, and we might as well agree we've found it.'

'He's been listening to us talk here,' Mullins said.

'Wonderful deduction,' said the Saint. 'I can see how you became such a successful detective. Too bad you made such an unsuccessful crook.'

Brine was licking his lips nervously, glancing at his daughter and Mullins.

'Templar,' he blurted. 'You're in this with us. You deserve a share. We'll split.' He smiled hopefully. 'How's that?'

'I agree that I deserve a share,' Simon said. 'Let's say something like a hundred per cent. I might send you a Christmas pudding in prison, though, if you'll tell me just when you decided to include me in your plans. Was it before or after you conned Drew into thinking you were on his daughter's trail?'

'You wouldn't believe it,' Mullins said, 'but we really were on to her trail—the real Mildred Drew's, I mean. So we made that deal with Drew to find her.'

'And then you couldn't produce,' volunteered the Saint, 'so you decided to find a substitute Mildred.'

'That was all my idea,' Phyllis said proudly, looking no less ingenuously wide-eyed than she had in her role of millionaire's daughter. 'And since they couldn't get anything for a Mildred who wasn't a Mildred, they had to pretend to kidnap her and get the money that way.'

'And you needed a go-between who didn't know Mildred,' Simon said. 'Some innocent sucker who'd think he was serving everybody's best interests by carrying messages and money.'

'Right!' said Phyllis brightly.

Brine's pride in the scheme was more apologetic.

'Of course we didn't plan to bring you into it till we just happened to hear your friend mention your name at a bar. Then we spotted you in the hotel, and...'

'And set up that performance where I was fishing,' said the Saint.

Brine and Mullins both nodded.

'The whole thing sort of ... developed, you might say,' Mullins put in. 'No offence intended.'

'We never went wrong before,' said Brine hopefully. 'We

were always straight, going towards our old age grinding through divorce investigations for twenty quid a week. I . . . I guess the temptation was just too much.'

'That might bring a tear to my eye,' Simon said, 'if I hadn't already used up my sympathy on Mildred's romantic problems. Now open the door there, and let my friend out.'

Pat Kelly's last outburst had died away after the reclosing of the heavy door, and it seemed doubtful that he could have heard what had been going on since. Mullins looked apprehensively at the door.

'He's . . . ah . . . pretty mad,' he said.

'Well, you won't mind that,' said Simon. 'Just throw the bolt and stand back. And Brine, you slide that case very gently across the floor in this direction.'

Brine hesitated, but the Saint gave him an encouraging waggle of his revolver, and then the detective obediently sent the attaché case scooting towards the exit. Mullins, in the meantime, with the tremulous caution of a demolition trainee defusing his first live bomb, was drawing back the bolt that held Pat Kelly prisoner.

That was when Phyllis dropped the lantern. The instant it shattered on the floor the wick went out and the place was blindingly dark. In the confusion of sounds and physical sensations, the Saint was aware that Pat had apparently charged out of his dungeon with such force and velocity that the massive door had swung wide and crashed back against the wall. It also seemed, judging from the accompanying crunch and groan, that Mullins had perhaps been flattened between the door and the wall like a hapless beetle caught in the pages of a rapidly slamming dictionary.

Simon yelled to identify himself to Kelly, and at the same time sensed from the shape of the bulk heaving itself at him out of the blackness that he was being attacked by Brine.

He neatly sidestepped and tripped the fat man, whose impetus carried him sprawling to the floor.

'Simon!' Kelly was shouting. 'Where are ye?'

'Grab the girl,' Simon said. 'Do you have a match?'

Kelly quickly produced a flame, which revealed two men unconscious on the floor, but no Phyllis. There was also no attaché case.

'She must have run out while I was tending to Brine,' Simon said. 'You watch these goons, I'll catch her.'

He hurried through the door, dodged around piles of stone, and heard the sound of the girl's running steps in the direction of the car. But he was too close behind to allow her any chance of starting the engine and pulling away. He had a glimpse of her jumping over some rocks and setting off at a dead run down the hillside.

Before he had chased her far she made the mistake of looking back over her shoulder to see whether or not he was gaining. She stumbled and fell violently head first, rolling several times but never loosing her grip on the case clutched against her chest.

She was lying face up, gasping for breath, when Simon arrived at her side.

'Hurt yourself?' he asked.

'My back,' she moaned. 'It's . . . I think it's broken.'

'They'll put it right for you in the prison hospital,' the Saint said sympathetically.

He bent down to help her, and she winced with pain as she started to raise herself. Simon saw the sudden movement of her right arm and averted his face to avoid most of the handful of earth she flung at him. Even so she managed to roll away, and dash off again. This time, though, he caught her before she had gone twenty feet and swung her around, making her drop the attaché case, and pinning her arms behind her.

'You want the money for yourself!' she cried. 'You're no better than the rest of us. In fact you're worse.'

'Worse?' asked Simon mildly.

'Yes.' Phyllis's big eyes suddenly welled with tears. 'They ... forced me to do it.'

'How?'

'My mother. She needs this dreadful operation. There's only one surgeon in the world who can do it. In America. And he charges ten thousand pounds.'

The Saint threw back his head and laughed.

'It's *true*!' said Phyllis. 'Really.'

'I'm afraid the stage lost a great star when you decided on a life of crime.'

Phyllis looked more genuinely upset than she had a moment before.

'Simon,' she said, 'you wouldn't ... really turn me in, would you?'

'Oh, yes. You're a very naughty girl.'

Her face crumpled, wet-eyed and kittenish.

'Please! I won't do anything wrong ever again, I swear. If you'll just let me go.'

Kelly was hallooing from the top of the hill, unable as yet to see where they were. Simon looked at Phyllis and loosened his grip.

'You promise you'll live a clean and decent life, devoting yourself to good works and never telling any lies?'

'Oh, I do! I promise!'

'All right, then.'

He let her go entirely. She was unbelieving.

'You mean?'

'Go on,' he said.

She stood on her tiptoes, gave him a swift kiss, and turned to run. As she passed the attaché case she snatched it up and took off down the hill like a rabbit.

'Don't try to spend any of that money, though,' Simon called after her. 'It's counterfeit!'

She stopped and turned.

'What did you say?' she shouted through clenched teeth.

'It's all counterfeit. Just bait to get your father to lead me here.'

The word she said then was not so impressive as the way she said it. She took the attaché case and hurled it to the ground. Then she ran and disappeared among the trees.

Simon went and knelt by the case, which had fallen open, spilling bundles of money—quite genuine Irish money—out on the ground. He made certain estimates of the value of his time, the expense of repairs to his car, and other worthy considerations, and stowed away what some less generous people might have considered a disproportionate number of the bundles of bills in his jacket pockets. But the Saint was an extraordinarily generous man, and he saw no reason to make an exception when being generous with himself.

Pat was coming down the hill.

'Are ye alone?' he called. 'Couldn't ye catch her?'

The Saint closed the attaché case and went to meet his friend.

'She's still running,' he answered.

'Ah, well, and I'm not sorry,' said Pat. 'She was a darlin' little thing. Led astray by her ould man.' He gestured towards the castle. 'Them's the two buzzards I'd like to take apart.'

'Are they all right?'

'They're trussed up so they couldn't give a flea any trouble. I've a throat as dry as a Bedouin's wit. What say we leave'm there to stew while we go get a spot o' somethin' to ease the pain?'

'We'd better bring them along,' Simon said. 'I'd like to

get in touch with Drew before he decides I've made off with the loot.'

'I wonder where his real daughter is?'

'I did some checking, and it seems she definitely flew to Mexico the day she disappeared from home. By now she's probably enjoying her honeymoon.'

'While we have our few days o' peace and freedom ruined chasin' after her all over Ireland,' said Kelly. 'Well, maybe we can get in a day o' fishin' anyway.' He scratched his chin, and gave Simon a sly sidelong glance. 'Still an' all, it's too bad that colleen Mildred, or Phyllis, or whativer her name really is, turned out to be such a naughty one. I'm thinkin' ye might have had more fun with her than with me.'

The Saint grinned pensively at the moon.

'It's a small world,' he said cheerfully. 'Maybe, one of these days, I will.'

II THE GADGET LOVERS

Adapted by Fleming Lee
　Original Teleplay by John Kruse

ONE

ORDINARILY the Saint concerned himself very little with rabbits, considering them—when he considered them at all—happy creatures hopping about fields, reputedly a plague to farmers, but cute subjects for greeting cards and Disney cartoons. He had not even devoted much thought to those bunnies of the nubile human kind who in recent years have established elegant burrows in cities all over the capitalist world.

Maybe it was the novel notion of bunnies in Berlin that brought Simon Templar to the unwonted but not unpleasant surroundings in which he found himself on a particular evening in late June. Three hours remained before the departure of his plane from Tempelhof. Why not sample the undoubtedly unique incongruities of the Berlin Bunny Club?

What Hefner had wrought, the world had bought—or, as in this case, borrowed. This was no franchised Playboy Club, but a free appropriation of some of their most publicized attractions, with local adaptations. Strange are the ways of the spread, and decline, of civilizations.

Ensconced comfortably at the dark bar, with long-limbed, bare-shouldered rabbits scurrying over the shadowy landscape, Simon had to admit that here, indeed, was something to stir the most cynical adventurer's sense of audacity: it was not just the female forms; invitingly outfitted as they were, they presented nothing particularly novel in the way of human anatomy. It was the idea of the thing—the magnificent impudence of the fact that this harem of lovely but purportedly untouchable hares should be dispensing American steaks, French wines, and voyeuristic enticements far out here on the eastern marches, within the very jaws of Asia, surrounded on every side by hundreds of miles of bleak collectivism.

But for all one could have known in the hermetic dimness of the West Berlin rabbit hutch, it might have been December outside instead of June, the remembered lights of the Kurfürstendamm might have been the neon of Manhattan, and the ugly concrete slabs of The Wall not many yards away might have been among the foothills of Rockefeller Center. Here inside, everything was all sweetness and dark—soft jazz, good whiskey, and mass-produced, sanitized eroticism.

The synthetic aspects were repellent to the Saint, who now that he'd tried the experience could think of approximately eight hundred better ways to spend his rare spare moments than sitting at a bar visually absorbing standardized sexuality which had about as much impact to it as the identical squares of butter set out on the dining tables.

He drained his glass and had just pulled his money from his pocket when his attention was arrested by the approach of a most luxuriantly developed young lady whose display included things of much greater charm than the cellophane-covered packets in the tray at her waist.

'*Zigaretten?*' she said. 'May I you serve?'

Simon handed her a note and accepted one of the packs.

'You serve very nicely.'

'Thank you, sir,' she said, smiling, and moved away.

Such an ordinary event would not be worth recounting, except that it is with such seemingly insignificant encounters that a wait for a plane can turn into an adventure.

If the cigarette bunny, in her mammary munificence, had not come along at just that moment, and if Simon had not turned to witness the oscillatory retreat of her pretty little bottom, made rabbit-like by a fascinating caudal appendage somewhat resembling an overgrown powder puff, he would not have noticed the iron-grey stocky man sitting alone at a table on the other side of the dance floor. Alone, at least, except for several bunnies who stood around laughing at some story he was telling.

Simon turned back to the bar and said almost absently to the white-jacketed young man behind it, 'Another of the same, please.'

It took surprisingly few seconds for him to isolate from the mass of faces in his memory even so relatively obscure a figure as William Fenton, ex-Royal Navy, more recently with British Intelligence. Simon's previous contact with him had been brief but friendly, and now he had to decide whether he wanted to—or ought to—renew the acquaintance. There was always the possibility that Fenton was involved incognito in some mission or other, and would not appreciate having his identity heralded all over bunny heaven.

'Here you are, sir.'

The bartender was blond and pale-eyed, and more notable for friendly efficiency than for lively conversation, which suited Simon fine. But, thanking him, he noticed a sudden change in the man's expression, a shift to new alertness. The grey eyes followed—as the Saint could see by glancing into the mirror-covered wall—the entrance and transit of a dark unattractive individual in a poorly cut suit.

The newcomer did what most newcomers to clubs do not do: having entered by the front door, he went more or less directly to the rear door, an obscure portal shrouded in black velvet, AUSGANG glowing above it, and disappeared behind the curtains.

Even a person less well versed in the ways of the ungodly than Simon Templar would have felt some suspicion by now that all was not precisely as it should be in this modern Wonderland. The hasty newcomer was no White Rabbit, but he was most certainly intent on meeting some sort of deadline, and he was choosing a strange route by which to do it.

The Saint had already gone beyond suspicion to active calculation. The eyes of the bartender became his mirror. The teutonic mixologist had become overly busy polishing glasses, but his narrowing gaze never left the velvet drapes of the exit.

When Simon whirled from his stool it was already almost too late. The dance had just ended, and the departing couples had opened a clear avenue from the exit door to William Fenton's table. Pushing slowly from between the black curtains was the blunt snout of a silencer.

Until that moment, the wine bunny had inadvertently shielded Fenton. Now she moved around his table to pour champagne, and there was no time for the Saint to call out a warning. In that space of precious breath or two which an ordinary man would have wasted staring helplessly, Simon acted.

A waitress was passing, carrying on her tray a gigantic platter of flaming shish kebab. In one, swift, fluid movement, like the blurred attack of a hawk, the Saint leaped forward, snatched up one of the long steel spears, dripping blue flame, and hurled it unerringly across the whole width of the room.

Like a blazing arrow it pierced the velvet curtains. A man screamed. Simultaneously the champagne bottle exploded, showering Fenton with foam and glass.

In the ensuing pandemonium, as the would-be assassin fell forward hopelessly entangled in smouldering draperies, Simon moved through panicking masses to the wine-drenched table. But there he found no gratefully uninjured William Fenton. He found no William Fenton at all—which was clearly impossible. So he lifted the edge of the tablecloth, stooped, and found himself looking straight into the unblinking eye of an automatic.

It was natural that the Saint's fame as a modern buccaneer should have made him vividly remembered by most of those who had had even transient contact with him. William Fenton hesitated only for a split second.

'Simon Templar! Of all people to be rescued by.'

The former naval officer crawled from under the table and put away his weapon.

'I assume it must have been you who put on the spear-throwing exhibition.'

'Who else?' drawled the Saint. 'There's just one infection I couldn't save you from, even though you seemed in imminent danger of succumbing.'

'What's that?' Fenton asked as they made their way past hysterically weeping bunnies to the fallen sniper.

'Tularemia?'

'Tularemia?'

'Rabbit fever.'

Three burly policemen had now arrived, and Simon remained at a discreet distance as they extracted the skewer from his victim's shoulder and the victim from the heavy velvet curtains. Then one of the officers proceeded to haul the wounded man across the room towards what the manager said was the nearest private place: the business office.

The second cop stayed by the exit, while the third blockaded the main entrance, doubtless in an effort to maintain the status quo until the arrival of higher authorities.

The Saint and Fenton went along to the office, having already been implicated by witness, and when the policeman had deposited his groaning burden on the zebra-skin sofa, he turned to them.

'*Nun, bitte*. One of you is the gentleman who threw the shish kebab at this man?'

'Ridiculous though it sounds,' Simon said in fluent German, '*Sie haben recht*. I did it.'

At that point Fenton interceded, showing a card.

'I am with the British embassy, and this gentleman saved my life. The situation is more involved than I am free to tell you. I would very much appreciate it if you would call Herr Gratz of your Special Branch and request in my name, as you see here on the card, that he come to this club at once.'

The policeman drew himself up with greater respect.

'*Jawohl*, Herr Fenton. But both of you gentlemen must remain here, please. No one is allowed to leave the building.'

'Of course,' Fenton said. 'But would you ask these other people to leave the room? It seems improper...'

'Understood, Herr Fenton. Naturally.'

A few moments later Simon and Fenton were alone with the sniper, who looked at them with understandable moodiness from beneath his weedy black hair.

'What is your name?' the intelligence officer snapped.

'Hahn.'

'Tell us what this is all about. And quickly.'

Hahn closed his eyes and compressed his lips. Fenton glanced around the room, which obviously had been got up to conform with certain magazine specifications of the ideal seduction chamber, even down to the drooling red and orange abstract painting over the fireplace.

Fenton took up a poker from the cold hearth.

'I'm not going to play around. Who is doing this, and why?'

Hahn opened his eyes, but did not answer.

'I'll use this on your shoulder. I'm not in the least squeamish.'

Hahn shrank back and gasped, 'Please. No. A man offers a job. I take it.'

'What man?' Fenton asked.

'A man in a bar, no doubt,' said the Saint, 'whose face and name you can't remember.'

'*Ja*,' Hahn agreed.

'Judging from your inexpert performance out there,' Simon said, 'I'm almost inclined to believe you.'

'Their lot have killed thirteen Russian intelligence agents in four months,' Fenton put in. 'They're trained assassins, not casual labour.'

Hahn turned his head away.

'I've put him on a skewer already,' said the Saint good-naturedly. 'I'd have no compunctions about roasting him. After all, he's a Hahn, and pretty foul to boot.'

'But let's pluck him first,' Fenton put in, shamelessly continuing the pun. He grasped the man's lapels and pulled him wincing to his feet. 'If you please, Simon.'

A brief but expert frisk revealed only one thing of interest: a two way transistor radio about the size of a cigarette box.

'Standard Russian equipment,' Fenton said, dropping Hahn back on to the sofa.

'Where'd you get it?' Simon asked.

'The man, he says when I finish the job I report back to him, with that.'

'Where is he?'

'I do not know.'

'Then report,' Fenton said, taking the radio and shoving it into Hahn's hand. 'Tell him I'm dead.'

Hahn was hesitant.

'Go on,' demanded Fenton.

'Neun zu sieben. Neun zu sieben. Antworten Sie, bitte.'

'Now if you'll excuse me for a second,' Simon murmured, 'I want to take a look through the door at a pal out here.'

He had felt sure that the police would not let the bartender wander far, and he was right. Without even leaving the doorway of the office, he could see the blond man occupying himself intently with something just below the counter. Behind Simon, Hahn was still intoning his numerical incantation.

'Neun zu sieben. Neun zu sieben.'

But then, as the bartender continued his operations, the Saint heard a soft electronic whine in the office behind him, rising in pitch and volume like the sound of an irate mosquito. He spun around.

'Fenton, run!'

He could see Hahn, puzzled, holding the radio away from his ear. Fenton was already diving for cover.

'Throw it away, man,' he was yelling. 'Into the fireplace! Fast!'

Simon escaped the blast with an agile move which put him just outside the door. The explosion was small in range but noisy and very effective. It had turned the unfortunate Hahn into an abstraction with little more recognizable form than the painting which now sagged at a rakish angle over the mantelpiece.

William Fenton picked his way through the smoke and debris.

'At last I've actually seen it happen.'

'Something you've been looking forward to?' asked the Saint. 'And people say radio's lost its punch.'

A policeman shoved his way through the newly gathered mob at the door and stared at the wreckage.

'We're all right,' Fenton said. 'But this man is not.'

'I see,' said the policeman, closing the door and hurrying to the body. 'What happened?'

'When Herr Gratz comes he will explain.'

'The bartender will already have escaped in the confusion, of course,' Simon said. 'But just in case, why don't you check on it?'

The policeman gave orders to a comrade as Fenton asked, 'The bartender?'

'Yes. He seemed to be twiddling with some gadget over at the bar at just about the time Herr Hahn went up in smoke. Now if you'd explain the background of these fireworks...'

'It's a part of a death campaign,' Fenton said. 'The organized assassination of intelligence agents.'

'By radio? Sort of a variation on the singing commercial?'

Fenton's sense of humour was perhaps more limited than the Saint's.

'Not only radios,' he went on. 'Explosive gadgets in general. All Russian espionage equipment.'

'But you said thirteen Russian agents had died. They knocking off their own men?'

'If I knew who was behind it, this might not have happened tonight.'

Fenton stooped and picked up the remnants of the radio, a tangled lump of metal.

'This isn't a timed device. It had to be triggered. An impulse beamed from outside, probably from very short range.'

'In this case from the bar, I'm sure. Shall we see if our friend left any traces there?'

Predictably, he had not.

'The bar man,' Simon said to the cigarette bunny. 'Where is he?'

'He left.'

'What is his name?'

'Klaus. Hans Klaus.'

'I would suggest that you put out a call for him,' Fenton said to the nearest policeman. 'All stations. The club will have his address. He certainly knows something about this.'

'*Ja*, Herr Fenton. I have spoken with Herr Gratz. *Er kommt schnell*. And he says you are to be allowed complete freedom of action.'

'Very good. When he arrives, tell him I and my friend will be at Dr. Mueller's laboratory. He knows where that is.'

'Mueller. *Jawohl*.'

Simon became aware that his arm was in the beefy grip of William Fenton, and that he was being towed through the door towards the street.

'I have a plane to catch,' he protested.

'You *did*,' Fenton said.

TWO

The laboratory of Dr. Friedrich Mueller was on Wittelsbacherstrasse. It had every appearance of an exceptionally clean radio repair shop. Neatly disembowelled, pocket-sized cases of various shapes and colours spilled their glassy and silvery innards on the counter tops. Manuals the size of telephone directories lay open to esoteric diagrams, and the walls were lined with tools and coils of wire.

But Dr. Mueller, for all the atmosphere of his laboratory, was considerably more enthusiastic about his work than most repairmen of any species. A tall man with keen blue eyes and closely cropped brown hair, he greeted Fenton with a brisk handshake.

'Dr. Mueller,' Fenton said, 'this is Simon Templar.'

The scientist's eyes enlarged with recognition as he extended his hand.

'*Ach*, the famous Saint. I am honoured.'

'Dr. Mueller works primarily with the West Berlin police,' Fenton explained, 'but in special cases he co-operates with us undercover people. And this is a special case.'

Mueller turned serious and nodded.

'So,' he said in careful, barely accented English, 'you actually have seen one explode? *Wunderbar*. Our theories facts are becoming. And was it as we thought?'

'Exactly,' said Fenton, 'but more powerful.'

'Yes. As it must be. We have ourselves not been idle. Except for the fact that we do not have the explosive, we have the reconstruction of the used-in-the-other-killings-devices managed.'

'Show us, please,' Fenton said.

Mueller picked up a small cigarette lighter from one of the tables.

'This. A little miracle. It will light cigarettes . . .'

He demonstrated the flame.

'Also will it pictures make. Nine of them. But on the tenth one, the last picture . . . boom! And the man who uses it is blown to pieces.'

Simon took the small metal case and turned it in his fingers as Mueller pointed out the details of its operation.

'The ideal gift for touring friends who like to show their snapshots,' Simon said. 'Amazingly little thing to do much damage.'

'But it does do much damage. The secret is a micro-explosive. Very small amount. Very powerful. We can only approximate it.'

'Which explains our vital interest in the whole thing,' Fenton said. 'Aside from the politics, I mean.'

'Have you seen one of these?' Mueller asked, picking up a briefcase.

'I assume it does something more interesting than contain papers,' Simon said.

'Naturally,' Mueller assured him with a broad smile. 'And this. A signet ring.'

He offered it to Simon, who politely declined.

'I'll leave such things to experts.'

'Very sensible,' said Mueller. He slipped the ring on to one of his fingers. 'Wearing this, I may the briefcase quite freely handle. The ring neutralizes the proximity fuse in the lock. But not wearing it, the heat of my hand would activate the fuse, and up would go the whole thing, taking me with it.'

'But with all apologies,' the Saint put in, 'isn't that approximately as new in espionage tactics as the old knife in the back?'

'Ah,' said Mueller agreeably, 'our friends, the unknown assassins, have a modification introduced. I will demonstrate. Gerda, please.'

Gerda, the Saint decided on seeing her profuse bulk lumber into the room, was not the modification introduced, unless the opposition had descended to the use of lady wrestlers. But while she would have offered no serious competition to a Mata Hari, she was quite useful, apparently, as a pack mule, and probably impervious to explosions.

On Dr. Mueller's instructions, she donned the signet ring and carried the lethal briefcase into an adjoining room which was separated from the main laboratory by a steel door. Through a small, very thick viewing window, the three men watched Gerda place the briefcase on a table in the centre of the bare-walled concrete chamber. She put the signet ring on top of the lock and left it there as she returned to Mueller's side, closing the heavy door behind her.

'So,' the scientist said, 'ordinarily the closeness of the ring to the fuse prevents any possible explosion. The unsuspecting spy goes happily along, little suspecting that anything can happen. Then, somewhere not far away, somebody one of these has.'

He waved what appeared to be a small transistor radio.

'A transmitter with a range of a few hundred yards. It will the neutralizing effect of the ring neutralize. Cancel it. *Kaput*. You understand?'

'*Jawohl, Herr Doktor*,' Simon said.

Mueller switched on the transmitter, which began to emit an almost inaudible low pitched whine gradually ascending in pitch and volume, uncomfortably reminiscent of the sound effects immediately preceding Herr Hahn's messy demise.

There was, of course, an explosion, a good deal less powerful and more smoky than the one at the Bunny Club, but quite satisfactory. It left the table a heap of kindling.

The men withdrew from the window as Gerda went through the steel door to clear away the debris.

'Counter-espionage *par excellence*,' the Saint said thoughtfully. 'But if I understand, Russian secret agents are being killed by their own gadgets—and not through any efforts of your people?'

'Right,' Fenton answered. 'But they claim that we're responsible, of course.'

'The next logical question is,' Simon continued, 'why *aren't* you responsible? I should think you'd be delighted to get rid of a few.'

Fenton looked mildly shocked.

'My dear fellow, if we kill their agents, they kill ours. It just isn't done. Except in the most extreme circumstances.'

'I see. And you're afraid that these unexplained explosions are going to lead to a wholesale vendetta.'

'Precisely. We know that Moscow is planning a revenge operation right now. One of the very very high-ups in their secret police is on his way to Berlin this minute.'

'Not the mysterious Colonel Smolenko?'

Fenton looked at the Saint in surprise.

'How could you know?'

'Smolenko seems to reserve himself for pulling the cord after somebody else has cranked up the guillotine. I've followed the MGB system a bit—enough to know who'd be most likely to be handling what. Smolenko's one of those second-generation Commies with a genius for survival no matter how often the leadership gets shuffled. Must be a pretty effective fellow.'

Fenton nodded glumly.

'And the more effective he is, the worse for our chaps.'

'Obviously,' Simon said to Mueller, 'it's very important to know who makes the originals of these devices. They come from Russia?'

'*Nein*. They do not. On the outside, they could come from anywhere. On the inside—the miniaturization is too fine to be Russian. We believe Russian manufacture is absolutely out of the question.'

'We must find out where it's from, if not Russia,' Fenton put in, 'and I don't mean next week. Smolenko passes through here in half an hour on the train to Paris.'

'Know what I smell?' asked Simon thoughtfully. 'Chop suey.'

Mueller looked baffled.

'Please?'

Simon pulled up the corners of his eyes, oriental style.

'The original inventors of gunpowder. I think they must be tossing a few exploding fortune cookies in your midst. What could suit them better than to have your men and the Russians at one another's throats?'

'You make sense, my friend,' Mueller said.

A telephone rang, and the scientist answered it.

'*Ja. Moment, bitte.* Herr Fenton—Herr Gratz is calling.'

'Fenton here. Oh . . . I see. Well, keep at it, anyway. He has to be involved somehow.'

'Klaus got away?' asked the Saint.

'Yes,' Fenton said, putting down the phone. 'They traced him from the club to the railway station and then lost him.'

'Smolenko,' the Saint said matter-of-factly.

Fenton's eyes flashed.

'My God, yes. And if Klaus is a trained killer—if he gets Smolenko ... we're in for it!'

Simon nodded towards the phone.

'Better put this in the hands of the regular authorities, don't you think?'

'The police? But nobody knows Smolenko. He'll be travelling under another name, probably with an escort of red herrings. We've got only twenty minutes. Could the police spot Klaus just from your description?'

Simon started to speak, then didn't. He could picture his hopes of non-involvement lifting even now from the earth of Free Berlin and winging their way west into the night with that plane he'd never catch.

'You're the only one of us who's had a good look at Klaus,' Fenton continued. 'There'll likely be two dozen blond men on that train somewhere near his age.'

'Now, Bill ...'

'Simon,' the intelligence officer said crisply, 'you've fifteen minutes to catch the Berlin–Paris Express. I'll stay behind here covering other eventualities.'

'Like the champagne at the Bunny Club.'

Fenton grinned.

'There are some things there that could stand closer scrutiny.'

'While I'm getting scrutinized by Rasputin's successor.'

'Come outside.'

Somehow or other Fenton already had a cab waiting at the door with its flag down, and he smiled at Simon's reaction to his confident efficiency.

'I felt sure you'd choose the proper course,' Fenton said.

The dash for the *Hauptbahnhof* was efficient too. In spite of screeching turns and roaring spurts down the straightaways, no one was killed, and they arrived at the station just on time. Simon sprinted across the loading area and jumped aboard the Paris-bound express just as it started to creak from its concrete slip.

But by that time any lingering nostalgia he might have felt for his earlier plans had been suppressed by the excitement that had begun to course through his blood. At the Bunny Club he'd been like an idling machine, cooling down between one strenuous trial and the next, but ready to move when the signal came. Now the signal had come, unexpectedly but unmistakably, and he was instantaneously co-ordinated, his senses keen, his nerves calm but alert, his whole body a magnificently operating unit.

The train was picking up speed, passing from under the huge canopy of the station's roof. The wheels rumbled smoothly underfoot, and the car swayed slightly. The few passengers who had been waving goodbye to friends from the corridor windows went into their compartments, and almost suddenly the entire population of the train seemed to settle into midnight somnolence.

Simon had, even in his haste, taken care to enter the train at the dividing point between the second- and third-class sections of the train. The third-class cars were at the rear, and there the unfortunate passengers would be nodding shoulder-to-shoulder on bare benches amid whimpering infants and greasy lunch bags. It seemed unlikely, however, that the guardians of the proletarian revolution would go quite that far to demonstrate their principles or even to achieve anonymity. The more luxuriantly upholstered and privately compartmented segments of the train were a much better bet. As for Klaus, he could be anywhere, assuming he was on the train at all, and he would most likely be surveying the same territory that Simon now proceeded to cover.

The Saint took on a sleepy, possibly somewhat alcoholic

air, and wove his way along the corridor peering through the window of each compartment with the amiably confused expression of a man who'd forgotten the location of his seat. To the few people who were awake enough or alert enough to notice him, he gave an apologetic smile as he passed on.

His task was, of course, complicated by the fact that he had no idea of the appearance of the Russians for whom he was searching. He could only hope that his experience and instincts would serve him as well as they had on many former occasions.

He covered three second-class cars and two first-class cars with no success. The street lights of the Berlin suburbs had long since been left behind, the checkpoint into Eastern Germany had been negotiated. In place of the city's brightness there was the black rural landscape, marked here and there by the glow of a village or town, blending with the inner reflections of the corridor windows.

Then the opening of the door of the next car forward produced hefty odours of wine, cigars, cigarettes, and beer, along with subdued sounds of revelry. Simon had entered the refreshment lounge, where an exhausted and rumpled waiter was dispensing goodies to a troupe of plump insomniacs in various stages of hilarity, gravity, or asphyxiation from cigar smoke.

At the extreme opposite end of the car was a familiar face whose slate grey eyes were looking startled at Simon through the haze. Simon looked at the face. It belonged to Hans Klaus.

The Saint tried to shove his way through the lounge car before Klaus could lose himself somewhere up ahead, but it was a little like trying to run unhindered through the last three minutes of a football match. First the waiter blocked the aisle, and then an extraordinarily broad-backed man with a size-twenty neck and a determined aversion to being pushed around.

By the time Simon arrived at the next car, a sleeper whose compartments had no windows facing the corridor, Klaus was just disappearing at the other end. In the next car, Simon hurried by two men who apparently, until the rapid passage of Klaus, had been resting their elbows on the lowered windows, enjoying the night air. They watched the Saint as he came to the end of his pursuit. The door at the end of the car was locked, and a sign in three languages told him: PASSENGERS FORBIDDEN: TRAIN CREW ONLY.

The little *toilette* to the Saint's left, which might have provided the last publicly available hiding place, was unlocked and empty. Simon looked back towards the two men who were observing him with sharp but controlled interest from their station halfway up the corridor. His main comfort at the moment was that if they were comrades of Klaus's they'd have been at his neck before this. There was no sign, in fact, that Klaus meant anything to them at all. On their faces—the one broad and red, the other somewhat triangular and pallid—was none of the overt alarm or amusement which might have been normally aroused by the scene they had just witnessed.

They offered no hints or comments. They just watched as if to see whether the so far harmless and mysterious little drama in which the Saint was involved might enlarge to include them—in which case their interest might become more active.

Their solemnity reminded Simon of the Secret Service men he had seen during appearances of American presidents—aloof, alert, and hair-triggered. He even thought he detected a bulge beneath the broad-faced one's broad-lapelled unstylish jacket.

No lightning thought processes such as the Saint's were

necessary to draw the essential conclusions. He had on his first quick trip down the corridor decided that these wakeful gentlemen were a very probable tip-off to the whereabouts of the fabled Colonel Smolenko. Neither of them possessed the aura of cleverness which would expectedly emanate from the Colonel himself.

Simon sauntered back along the corridor. When he came abreast of the two sentinels, who made no pretence of not staring at him, he stooped all of a sudden and squinted out the window as if he had seen something startling.

That was sufficient to distract his travelling companions long enough for him to open the compartment door they were guarding, step inside, and instantly throw the bolt.

The Saint did not need to understand much Russian to disentangle the frightened word *tovarishtch* from the heavy pounding of fists on the door.

He turned to see his prize, and for once even Simon Templar was momentarily at a loss: Colonel Smolenko seemed to be a woman.

THREE

SHE looked at him coolly from her seat by the window: lovely Slavic cheekbones, fine lips devoid of make-up, and such large brown eyes that the fact she was pointing a pistol at Simon seemed entirely anticlimactic. If her dark hair had been less tightly pulled to the back of her head, and if she had worn something more fetching than a raincoat which probably had relatives among the nearest circus tents, she could have competed on all points with the distracting rabbits of the Berlin Bunny Club.

'Open the door,' she said in English, gesturing with her automatic.

'I'm here to help you,' said Simon. 'Pardon me if I seem to gape, but I wasn't expecting a woman.'

'Does it matter?'

'It could matter very much under certain circumstances.'

'Keep your hands away from your body and turn and open the door.'

Her English was strongly accented but clearly pronounced, and her determination that Simon should obey her more or less promptly or have his liver ventilated was just as clear.

He unlocked the door and immediately was in the ungentle hands of the Russian Secret Police.

'What you do here?' the big one asked, pinning the Saint's arms behind him as the other despoiled his pockets of wallet, keys, and even small change.

Simon spoke to the beautiful colonel.

'I've come to warn you that there's a man aboard this train who very likely intends to see you dead before you reach Paris.'

'There are many men who intended to see me dead and ended up dead themselves,' she said with cold arrogance.

'I don't doubt that in the least. My compliments.'

Smolenko put down her pistol and lay aside the book which had fallen to her lap when her compartment was invaded. She took the passport which the smaller guard offered her from the Saint's jacket pocket.

'I think I do not need to look,' she said, with the most frosty trace of a smile. 'Simon Templar.'

The Saint responded with a more friendly smile of his own. He bowed his head slightly.

'I'm flattered that news of my infamy has spread as far as the Kremlin.'

'I have a photographic memory, and in our central office we have constantly updated files which inform us of the movements of any persons of interest who are in the area where I am going.'

'It's nice to be of interest, Colonel.'

The grip which the burly guard kept on Simon's arms was beginning to become irritatingly uncomfortable. The Saint knew a swift motion which would not only break the hold but send the holder to the hospital for a month, but that did not seem the best strategy for maintaining this temporary thaw in the Cold War.

'Do you mind if I stand up by myself?' he asked mildly. 'As you can see, I have no weapons.'

'Ivan,' the colonel said to the big guard, and continued in Russian.

Simon was freed, and he rubbed circulation back into his muscles. Ivan stationed himself at the door while his smaller, triangular-faced colleague produced a pistol that somehow seemed much too big for him and kept it pointed at the Saint.

'You may not leave,' Smolenko said. 'No one is to know who I am.'

'I have no desire to leave,' responded Simon with exaggerated gallantry. 'Such congenial company? Such heavy artillery? Besides, now there are enough of us for a rubber or two of bridge.'

'Sit down,' Smolenko said. 'Before you are killed, we must talk a little. Ivan, go order some tea.'

Ivan stared dubiously at his chief. Smolenko said something to him in Russian, and he shrugged and left the compartment. The other man took up the watch at the door. Simon was still standing.

'Now,' Smolenko said. 'Sit down. *Vis-à-vis.*'

'I prefer *tête-à-tête*,' said Simon, 'but you're the hostess.'

He sat down opposite her, crossed his legs, and relaxed. The comely colonel kept her eyes fixed on his face but showed no particularly urgent interest in anything he might have to reveal.

'You could have Raskolnikov there put away his hatchet,' Simon said finally. 'As I told you, I'm here for the sole purpose of saving your life.'

'His name is Igor, and I give the orders, and I have no need of anyone to save my life.'

'Apparently not, but don't you ever consider taking well-intended advice?'

'From bourgeois agents? Hardly.'

Simon looked pained.

'Sticks and stones may break my bones . . .'

'I do not understand.'

Obviously, she did not like not understanding.

'It's just a saying. You really speak English very well.'

'Anything it is necessary to do should be done well.'

'A very sound maxim.'

Ivan returned, spoke in Russian to Smolenko, and then—with bear-like pride in his linguistic achievements—addressed Simon in English.

'Tea come.'

'Excellent,' said the Saint. 'And well spoken.'

Ivan's ruddy countenance softened a little.

'Thanks you.'

'You're quite welcome.'

The four rode in silence for what must have been a mile or two, and all the time Smolenko just looked at him. The first step in some Asiatic method of wearing him down? Or was she searching the files of her photographic memory for information about him?

There was a soft knock at the door.

'Tea,' said Ivan, and reached for the handle.

'Wait,' Smolenko broke in. 'We must give a tip, I think.'

She thumbed through her book.

'Despicable bourgeois practice. In lieu of social justice you give measly alms.'

'Measly alms,' Simon repeated admiringly. 'That's very good. But you must get over this thing about the bourgeoisie. They're really very clean, industrious people. Salt of the earth, and all that jazz. Tipping isn't their idea of fun—it's the proletariat that insists on it.'

'The official recommendation is one mark,' the Colonel announced coldly.

She produced a coin purse, inspected both sides of a pfennig, closely examined a big five-mark piece. Simon reached over and selected a silver mark.

'There.'

She flushed slightly, and Igor, who had started forward, relaxed.

'Now,' she said.

Igor opened the door, and a white-coated waiter came in with the tray, bending quickly down to set it on a stand beside the door.

Simon was on him in an instant, one arm like a vice at his throat, the other twisting the man's wrist behind him.

'Meet Hans Klaus, bartender extraordinary,' the Saint said through grimly clenched teeth. 'Lock the door and search him. Hurry.'

'For why?' cried a dumbfounded Ivan.

But the urgency in Simon's voice was unmistakable, and the Russian began to pat down the feebly struggling captive.

'Bartender?' Smolenko said, showing the closest thing to perturbation she had allowed herself since the Saint's arrival. 'What is it you are doing?'

'Klaus is an unusual bartender. He's probably much more at home mixing Molotov cocktails than martinis.'

Ivan's search produced a transmitter device exactly like that demonstrated so effectively by Dr. Mueller in his laboratory.

'Quickly,' Simon said. 'Check the tea ... the tray ... inside the pot.'

Ivan obeyed despite his mystification, and within seconds discovered a small cone-shaped object which had been attached by suction under one edge of the tray. Suddenly Klaus darted out his hand and flipped the switch on the transmitter which Igor was holding. It began its now familiar thin crescendo.

'The window!' Simon yelled, twisting Klaus's arm until he yelped. 'Throw it out. Fast.'

Ivan slammed down the window and tossed out the little cone. Igor threw the transmitter. A second later there was an explosion which undoubtedly disturbed the dreams of a number of passengers about one car back.

'See what I mean about this fellow?' Simon said. 'Dispenses good cheer wherever he goes.'

Colonel Smolenko, who had been on her feet since the discovery of the bomb, stared at Klaus.

'He is the one you said would kill me?'

'*One* of the ones, probably.' With his lean strength he evoked a new whimper from Klaus and said to him in German, 'Now, tell us all you know, or I shall let these Russians tear you to pieces. Who are you working for?'

'A man ... in Paris.'

'His name?'

'*Ich weiss nicht.* I have him never seen. My orders come by telephone.'

'What orders?'

'Hahn to kill. Then this train to catch and the occupants of this compartment to kill.'

Simon released the erstwhile bartender, who rubbed his aching arm and took a deep breath.

'A nice night's work,' said the Saint, turning to Smolenko. 'Did you get all that?'

She nodded, and at the same moment Klaus grabbed the emergency stop cord. The train gave a tremendous lurch as the air brakes slammed on automatically. All those in the compartment except Klaus, who had prepared himself, went staggering off balance, and Smolenko fell back against the wall and slipped to the floor.

Klaus was out and running down the corridor. Igor and Ivan plunged after him. Their silenced shots were lost in the groans and rattles of the halting train.

The Saint knelt over Smolenko, who was limp on the carpet, her eyes closed. He picked her up to put her on the seat, already assured that she was not more than stunned.

Her eyelids fluttered, and she gave a sighing moan through parted lips.

'You look much more sweetly feminine asleep than awake, Colonel,' Simon murmured.

She opened her eyes wide.

'Put me down. Instantly!'

He dropped her ungently on to the seat, flat on her back.

'As you say, Colonel.'

She swung her legs around and stood up, jerking wrinkles out of her coat, trying to overcome dizziness with determined dignity.

'That was not good of you,' she snapped.

'Picking you up or putting you down?'

'Neither. I need no help. You insult me.'

'I'm not particularly flattered myself, Sonya. You couldn't have looked more horrified if you'd found yourself in the arms of King Kong himself.'

'My name is not Sonya, and I do not understand all your idioms. Please...'

'Please what?' Simon asked politely, after she had hesitated for several seconds.

She was apparently unable to think of any useful orders to give him. He had proven his value and the sincerity of his desire not to see her killed. But there was no trust in her eyes, only a touch of confusion behind the hard glaze of the secret police officer. She was spared having to manufacture a statement by the return of her bodyguards.

'They shot him dead,' she translated for the Saint. 'They placed his body in the water of the ditch before the train was fully stopped, and they told that the signal of this rope was a mistake.'

'Very clever,' Simon said with disgust. 'Why so quick

with the guns? Klaus might have led us to the ringleaders of the whole plot.'

'Whose plot?' asked Smolenko.

'The agents of yours who've been killed.'

Smolenko looked surprised.

'Our secrecy is apparently not good. You and this Klaus have both found me here, who am supposed to be a cultural exchange representative, and now you know all about the murders of our . . .'

She stopped herself.

'But you tell me, Mr. Templar. What is your part in all this?'

'I would say, in the first place, that your remark about secrecy is the understatement of the century. You couldn't have a bigger following if you had hired P. T. Barnum as a publicity agent. Which leads me to believe, as they say in the old films, that this whole deal is an inside job.'

'But what do you know, Mr. Templar? What facts do you have? What is your part in this?'

He told her, and she listened with more and more intense interest.

'So,' he concluded, 'these people—whoever they are—have managed to gain control of the production of your miniaturized equipment. You should know considerably more about that than I do. For instance, where do you get all those little toys like cigarette lighters that take pictures?'

'They are purchased in Western Europe by our Paris organization, which is absolutely trustworthy. You are lying. I am trying to think why.'

The Saint gave a weary sigh.

'Okay. Believe what you like. I'm only trying to help. If you get yourself blown into pretty little pieces in Paris, don't expect any flowers on your grave from me.' He stood up. 'Charming as your company is, I'm tired. I didn't ask for this job in the first place, and if anything happens to you now, you can't claim it's my fault.'

'Wrong,' Igor said, speaking English for the first time. 'We *are* blame you.'

'No person in Paris know Colonel Smolenko,' Ivan explained laboriously. 'Not what she is looking like...'

'Or that she is woman,' said Igor.

He prodded the Saint's shoulder with a long, skinny finger.

'Nobody know ... but you. So if she dies, it will be through you. But she will not die.'

Ivan looked cheerfully at the Saint and drew his broad peasant face closer.

'*You* will die.'

'A fall from the train?' Igor asked.

'*Da*. I am think yes.'

Smolenko's icy voice sliced Ivan's grin in half.

'Be silent, both of you.'

She looked thoughtfully at the Saint.

'Of course we could never let you go. Now, you say Smolenko will be killed?'

'I do indeed, unless you take precautions, including some kind of co-operation with Western intelligence.'

'Well, we will see if that is true, without co-operation of bourgeois spy apparatus. With your co-operation only. When we get to Paris in the morning...'

The Saint watched suspiciously as her lips pouted slightly in a smile.

'Yes?'

'We change places,' she said. 'I become your secretary, and you ... you become Colonel Smolenko.'

FOUR

Simon Templar had seen Paris many times, and in many seasons, but never as a colonel of the Soviet Secret Police, and never in quite such precarious circumstances.

The hotel was not exactly of the class he would have chosen either, but apparently it impressed red travel agents as striking the proper tone between capitalistic extravagance and unbecoming shoddiness. His own taste ran to such palaces as the George V, where he could treat himself to the level of luxury that he felt any self-respecting buccaneer deserved, but he realized that Smolenko might have to conform to a more ascetic expense account.

Of all the more gracious hostelries he had frequented, however, he could not recall one that he had entered with such an entourage. In addition to a pair of bellboys, there were Igor and Ivan lumbering along the thinly carpeted hallway on either side of him like a movie gangster's bodyguards, and Simon's new secretary, the former Colonel Smolenko, looking decidedly mussed by the long train journey, but still more attractive than she had any right to be, considering her almost total disdain for the civilized amenities which women ordinarily find indispensable for any sort of decent public appearance.

As the hotel employees opened the unimpressive suite, Igor and Ivan hurried inside and began inspecting the three bedrooms, the baths, and the closets. The porters went away looking surprised at the size of Simon's tip.

'Please,' Ivan said, dragging two straight chairs to the centre of the living room. 'Down.'

Colonel Smolenko sat in one of the chairs, half smiling at Simon's mystification.

'They want us out of the way while they search,' she explained. 'What you call, I think, standard operation procedure.'

The Saint watched as the security agents pulled out drawers, looked behind pictures, peered and felt under table tops and rugs.

'Do a thorough job, boys,' he said encouragingly. 'From now on practically anything you touch could go bang.'

'They are experts,' Smolenko said frostily. 'They need no advice.'

'You forget, darling,' Simon said, '*I* am in command now. I need no advice from a mere secretary, especially one who probably can't even take shorthand.'

'Mr. Templar . . .'

'Colonel to you. You communists carry this equality business much too far.'

Smolenko's lips tightened for a moment.

'You ask for trouble.'

'I have trouble, and I didn't ask for it. As a matter of fact, it occurs to me that as long as we're the same person we may as well be friends. Any objection to that?'

Smolenko simmered for another few moments, breathed deeply, and shook her head.

'I'm glad you're so understanding,' the Saint continued. 'After all, I'm not a philanthropist in any ordinary sense of the word, but what I'm doing is entirely for your own good.'

She gave an uncertain jerk of her head.

'You doubt me?' he asked. 'You have good reason to. As a matter of fact I'd have been gone long before this if I could have managed to contact someone to pass the job on to.'

'My men would have stopped you.'

'Don't tempt me to take that as a dare.'

There was an awkward silence. Simon stretched his long legs and yawned.

'I can't even think of anything I might be able to steal,' he said gloomily.

'Naturally you would think in terms of the profit motive,' Smolenko said.

He nodded agreeably.

'Of course.'

There was no sound for a while but the pushings and pullings and probings of the security twins.

'Have you been in Paris before?' Simon asked finally.

'No.'

'You'll be out shopping for clothes, I imagine, while I'm tracking down the manufacturers of those noisy cigarette lighters.'

'Why?'

'Well, women tend to associate Paris with fashions—and you surely can't be intending to go around *this* city in *that* coat.'

She flushed and smoothed the rumpled material.

'In ordinary circumstances a man would not dare to speak to me in that manner.'

'Would you send him to Siberia, or have him shot?'

'You think we are barbarians, don't you?'

'Not necessarily. I just think you have poor taste in clothes.'

'Clothing I regard as necessary covering to maintain body temperature. That is its only use.'

'Then I'd love to spend a couple of weeks with you on a South Sea island.'

Igor was taking a vase of roses apart, looking inside each

blossom. Finding nothing, he threw the whole bouquet out the window.

'Not a nature lover, your friend,' the Saint commented.

'He is trained to distrust all manifestations of bourgeois sentimentality.'

'Here we are back to your favourite subject again.'

'All good, *polkovnik*,' Igor said pointedly addressing himself exclusively to Smolenko.

'Fine,' Simon replied. 'Now you boys may unpack your suitcases and ...'

There was a tap at the door. Simon smiled with anticipation.

'The champagne.'

Smolenko looked horrified.

'Champagne?'

'I ordered it when we checked in.'

Ivan and Igor dashed for the door and stood on either side of it. Ivan yanked it open. The startled waiter blinked, then stepped hesitantly inside. Simon indicated the most convenient table, where the waiter put down the ice bucket and glasses, rattling the crystal when he heard the door slammed and locked behind him.

'*Voilà, m'sieu*,' he said nervously.

'Open it, please,' the Saint said in French.

'*Oui, m'sieu.*'

The waiter eased the cork towards release, looking more and more uneasy as the other occupants of the room moved several yards away from him.

'If you please, *m'sieu*, is something wrong?'

'We shall see,' said Simon. 'Open the bottle.'

At the pop of the cork everyone in the room except the Saint, who had long ago learned to control such easily anticipated reflexes, gave an undignified jump. The waiter's forehead was glistening with perspiration. He splashed a little of the Bollinger into a glass and offered it to the Saint. The Saint offered it to Smolenko, who gestured towards Ivan, who yielded to Igor. Simon handed the glass to the waiter.

'You taste it.'

'*Moi, m'sieu?*' the man asked, astounded.

'*Oui. Vous.*'

'*Merci, m'sieu.*'

The waiter took a sip and managed a sickly smile.

'All of it,' said Simon, touching the base of the glass with a fingertip.

The waiter drained it, then stood trying to preserve some semblance of nonchalance as four pairs of eyes studied his every twitch.

'That is all,' the Saint told him at last. 'You may go now.'

When Ivan opened the door, the waiter hurried out with relief. Simon filled the glasses as Igor gave the tray and the bottom of the bottle a close inspection.

'Cheers.'

Smolenko raised her glass grudgingly.

'This is generous of you.'

'You're very kind, but I'm not paying for it.'

'Who is?'

'The Kremlin, of course. We're on an expense account, aren't we?'

Smolenko glared at him.

'Your file is quite correct. You are nothing but a mercenary adventurer.'

'And one who likes staying alive. While we're dawdling merrily here, evil wheels are turning in this city. Your rather spectacularly defective electronic equipment is purchased from Paris. Klaus said he was hired here, by a man who knew the number of your compartment. If they were confident enough not to be watching the train when it arrived, they'll be suspicious when Klaus fails to report—so all in all our best course is to trace them before they trace us.'

'I am ahead of you,' Smolenko said. 'Someone will be here soon.'

'Who?'

'One of our best people. And now I take a shower and change clothes.'

'Remember, we're not in Moscow. You won't need much to maintain your body temperature.'

The desk called twenty minutes later, and Igor said *da*, hung up, called to Smolenko in Russian, and said to the Saint, who emerged from his bedroom straightening his tie: 'Blagot here.'

Smolenko came from her room and joined them, wearing a most plainly cut brown dress and cumbersomely heeled shoes which in the Western nations would rarely have been inflicted on any woman under sixty-five.

'I must admit,' Simon said, 'that for a female with the whole sartorial deck stacked against her, you manage to look amazingly beautiful.'

'I suggest you stay in your room,' she said.

'I suggest that as Colonel Smolenko, I'd better be here to greet our trusted friend. And I also suggest that you fill me in on who he is.'

'He is Blagot, a member of our Paris apparatus. I shall let him know who I am. We need no masquerade for him.'

'You've met him?'

'No. Nobody here has seen me.'

'Your naïveté is most affecting. Weren't you listening to what I said a few minutes ago? Your assassination was planned by someone who knew your entire programme. The higher a man is in your organization the more possible it is that he could be behind the whole thing. Now if you seriously want to relieve me of my starring role in this farce, I'll slip quietly away down the fire escape and leave you to your fate.'

There was a respectfully soft rap at the door.

'Stay,' Smolenko said to the Saint.

'Then let me handle this. Ivan, open the door.'

Ivan hesitated, looking towards Smolenko for confirmation. She nodded, and the bodyguard released the latch.

'Come in,' Simon said in French.

A rather short thick man, reminiscent of a greasy sausage in a black suit, entered the room and looked obsequiously and searchingly from face to face. But his personal appearance and mannerisms were completely overshadowed for the Saint by the adornment and contents of his right hand. The signet ring he wore, and the briefcase he carried, could have been identical twins of those Simon had seen exploded in Dr. Mueller's laboratory.

The mere fact that he had the items with him was no proof of murderous intentions. The ring and briefcase were standard equipment. Colonel Smolenko of all people would be aware of that. The teaser was in the question whether or not there was some as yet unknown but highly interested party lurking somewhere within a few hundred yards ready to send a signal which would override the neutralizing power of the ring and blast Suite 502 to kingdom come.

'Colonel Smolenko?' the newcomer asked.

'Comrade Blagot,' said Simon.

Blagot threw his fist up in the communist salute.

'On behalf of us all, welcome, comrade.'

'Thank you,' the Saint responded, pretending a slight difficulty with French pronunciation which ordinarily did not mar his fluent use of the tongue. 'My secretary, Comrade Malakov. Our security men . . .'

Blagot made his obeisances to each.

'And now,' Simon continued, 'how goes it?'

'The situation grows worse by the hour, Colonel. Another of our men died yesterday—in Liverpool, England.'

'An explosion?'

'Yes. But the cause...'

Blagot shrugged and distended his thick lips.

'I do not consider that an adequate answer,' Simon snapped with sudden harshness.

'Defective equipment, perhaps...' began Blagot.

The Saint moved threateningly towards him.

'If that remark is meant seriously, it indicates that the most defective equipment is in your brain, my friend.'

Blagot backed away a few paces, looking openly frightened.

'Some have talked of defective equipment, comrade, but I do not believe it. Naturally, the answer must be that British or American agents are planting bombs in the luggage of our people. That much is clear already.'

'One thing is clear to me already,' the Saint said, 'and that is that the handling of this affair by your department borders on total incompetence. For example, if you had even the smallest grasp of the true situation you would not have brought one of those briefcases here.'

'But Colonel Smolenko, I have made certain that it is empty of any harmful devices.'

'It contains its own explosive charge, does it not?'

'Naturally, but the ring...'

'The ring is useless against the saboteurs,' Simon said. 'Give that to me.'

Blagot set down the leather case and pulled off the ring, which the Saint put on his own finger. Then Simon took the briefcase to a table by the window and worked over it for a moment with a letter opener.

'What are you doing?' Smolenko demanded harshly, and then in reaction to Blagot's astonished stare she moderated her tone and asked with much more respect, 'Do you need help, Colonel? You frighten us.'

'I have finished already,' Simon said. 'I have simply broken the connection between the firing device and the explosive. Now we can speak without fear of violent interruption.'

He turned suddenly on Blagot, peering at him with intense eyes that were all blue ice.

'Comrade, tell me. Who in our organization knew the details of my trip to Paris?'

'Me. And of course Claude Molière.'

'Ah, yes. I have read his file. Nobody else?'

'Naturally not, Colonel. Your orders were that we maintain top security.'

'Which was not maintained.'

'It is unpardonable, Colonel, but...'

Blagot gave another of his shrugs and protruded his lips. Simon felt a desire to step on him as he would a cockroach. His moment of bloody fantasy was interrupted, however, by a thin, high-pitched sound—a sound he had expected as surely as he would have expected day to follow dawn.

'Here,' he said quickly, pointing to the table on which the briefcase lay.

They gathered around, all but Simon staring, perplexed. The faint little whine grew higher and louder until its pitch almost rose above human hearing. Then the room was abruptly silent.

'At that moment when the sound stopped,' the Saint explained, 'we would all have been blown into small pieces.'

He watched with satisfaction as the effect of his somewhat exaggerated description of the explosive's power registered on the semicircle of faces. Then he went on to explain the means by which such devastating effects were achieved.

Comrade Blagot mopped his oily brow with an unclean handkerchief.

'But it is impossible that anyone could have tampered with this case. I received it only today from our supplier.'

'No one needed to tamper with it,' the Saint said firmly. 'The radio signal receiver was built into it. And the same with the lighter-cameras and the miniature communications equipment. Now I think I shall pay a call on your supplier.'

'But the purchaser is a reliable man. I cannot believe that Molière . . .'

'Where is this Molière?' asked Simon.

'But, Colonel, you said you had read his file.'

'I read many files.'

'But Claude Molière is Assistant Controller for the whole *département*.'

'Imbecile! I mean where is he now, at this very moment?'

Blagot was properly abashed.

'I am sorry, my Colonel. I believe he should be at his shop. Let me telephone to make sure.'

'No. I should prefer to pay him a visit unannounced. And if I were you I would not be so quick to defend him. He may be a simple dupe, like yourself. On the other hand it is possible that he was standing somewhere down on the street broadcasting the request that this bomb blast us to our deaths.'

Blagot gulped.

'So now,' Simon announced, 'you will take us to your friend, Molière. If you please.'

FIVE

'Oh, brave old world, that hath such creatures in it.' Such was Simon Templar's reflection on his first view of Molière's Musique à Go-Go. The small narrow shop was a churning three-dimensional kaleidoscope of squirming and twitching teen-agers in boots, lavishly bell-bottomed trousers, mini-skirts, yellow checked jackets, and Edwardian neckwear. Like victims of tarantism, they could not rest even in a place which was not meant for dancing but for the sale of phonograph records. The savage sounds which moved them issued from three auditioning booths in the rear of the store, each screaming out the agony of a different disc. On the walls hung electric guitars, bongos, radios, and television sets. A couple of exhausted female clerks had apparently long ago given up trying to keep any kind of order, and contented themselves with watching the door in an effort to keep anybody from stealing anything.

Blagot shoved his way through the jerking crowd towards an office which looked out on the rest of the shop through a large window. Simon took Smolenko's hand to pull her up ahead of him when it appeared they would be separated in the crush. It was a surprisingly soft, warm hand, but it abruptly denied him the pleasure of any prolonged contact.

Ivan was so fascinated with the mini-skirts that Igor had to be sent back to fetch him through the mob.

'Colonel Smolenko,' Blagot said to Simon, ushering him into the little office, 'allow me to present Comrade Claude Molière.'

If Molière had believed that the Smolenko party had been recently despatched by a radio-controlled bomb, he did not betray the fact. Unfortunately, it was most likely that he would have been aware of the failure by now in any case. He was a birdlike man of about thirty-five, with a hooked beak and glittering black eyes, and his twittering nervousness seemed more a permanent characteristic than the result of a surprise confrontation.

'Colonel, Colonel,' he said, jumping to his feet and extending a moist, delicate hand, 'what a pleasure. What an honour.'

The Saint shook the hand coolly.

'My secretary, Comrade Malakov.'

'Comrade.'

'Comrade,' said the real Smolenko without enthusiasm.

Simon motioned her to one of the wooden chairs.

'My men will remain outside,' he said with a wry smile, 'keeping an eye on the quaint diversions of your country.'

'My apologies, Colonel. At least in here the sound is not deafening.'

'It does not matter. I am a man of few words and good hearing. I am sure you have many more interesting things to tell me than I could possibly tell you.'

Molière almost visibly squirmed before the threatening steel points of the Saint's eyes.

'Ah, Colonel, no,' he protested deprecatingly, looking as if he would have liked to change the subject entirely.

Simon was kind enough to help him. Glancing around the room, his eyes had settled on a bottle of a curiously spiralled shape which stood on a shelf between piles of catalogues.

'*Grand Abrouillac*,' Molière said observantly. 'A most distinguished liqueur which may be new to you.'

'I know of it,' said Simon, studying the label. 'It does not travel. I was not aware that it was ever exported from Switzerland.'

'You are a connoisseur,' Molière said with approval. 'A business friend supplies me. Damaged though it may be from its trip down the Alps, you may be surprised at its quality. May I pour you a glass? And your charming secretary, of course.'

'Thank you, no. We have just had champagne at our hotel.'

'Ah, Colonel,' Molière gushed, winking, 'champagne. You know how to live.'

'I try,' said the Saint. 'It seems to be increasingly difficult these days.'

Molière, feeling the pressure applied once more, shrivelled a bit. His laugh was weak.

'And now,' Simon said brusquely, 'to business. In Moscow we were struck—I might almost say shattered—by the excellence of your miniaturized equipment. Do you make it yourself?'

Molière hesitated, almost stammered.

'Uh . . . no.'

'Who does?'

'Ah . . . the firm of Grossmeyer, Cardin et Fils. Of Zurich.'

'Zurich. Good.'

Simon turned to Smolenko.

'Malakov, what was that thing we liked so much but had a little difficulty with—the lighter or the . . .'

'The lighter that takes pictures?' Molière interrupted. 'A charming toy. It has given you difficulties?'

'One could hardly call them difficulties.'

Simon waited to see whether his ambiguous statement would bring additional sweat to the shop owner's brow. It did. Then he went on:

'A tendency to jam temporarily after several exposures. These things are not my field. They are handled on a lower level. But as long as I am here I thought...'

'Colonel, I am sure the difficulties of which you speak must have involved only a single defective item or so. Our tests...'

'We cannot afford even one defective item. I trust you will see to the prevention of such oversights from now on.'

'Certainly, Colonel. Absolutely.'

'May I please have one of the photographic lighters?' the Saint asked.

'Now?' asked Molière with surprise.

'Yes. Now. If you please.'

'But of course,' Molière said with a notable mixture of facial expressions. 'One moment.'

He reached into one of the drawers of his desk and fumbled about as Simon turned and watched the display of rocking bodies which crammed the outer room. The Saint's mind was running in top gear, and his every move was calculated.

'Here, Colonel. With my compliments.'

'Thank you,' Simon said, taking the little burnished steel rectangle. 'Is it ready for use?'

'Oh, yes. It is loaded. Ten exposures. You can make a record of your travels.'

'And also test the possibility of faults in the mechanism.'

'Certainly.'

The Saint aimed the camera at Molière and pressed the tiny spring button in the hinge of the lid. Molière fidgeted and laughed.

'But, Colonel, is it wise? Photographs of me and my shop in your camera?'

'I shall not lose it.'

He took a picture of Smolenko, then he turned in his chair and made two shots of the dancing crowd beyond the window. He turned back and clicked the device again in Molière's direction. Molière blanched.

'The light here is poor,' he said.

'An espionage camera which will not make photographs in ordinary room light?' Simon asked incredulously. 'That would be inexcusable. Let us try it out there.'

Molière looked relieved until he discovered that 'out there' meant the main room of his shop. Simon snapped Blagot, who seemed to have no fear of the camera and was obviously quite happy to let his comrade, Molière, remain the centre of the testy Colonel Smolenko's attention. The genuine Smolenko appeared bored and vaguely disgusted at the inexplicable antics of her impersonator.

'Anti-capitalist propaganda,' said Simon cheerfully, taking a frame of the dancers. '*Fantastique.*'

'I have some other equipment to show you,' offered Molière nervously. 'Very interesting.'

'Not as interesting as this bizarre spectacle, surely. Just one moment. When I have finished the roll.'

Turning for his next shot, the Saint muttered to Igor in English, pushing him firmly in the direction of the back of the shop.

'Watch that door. Stop Molière if he tries to get away.'

The choreomaniacs were reaching heights of rhythmic abandon rarely seen north of Nigeria. It was quite understandable that a travelling Russian should want to preserve a few images of such exotic native customs with which to regale the folks back home. But Comrade Molière did not seem to sympathize with the desire. His dislike of the whole business became more and more obvious as Simon counted off his photographs.

'Almost finished now. Eight . . . nine . . .'

The Saint did not exactly see Molière run for the rear of the shop. Like a startled bird, the terrified man was halfway out of sight before anyone saw him move. Simon watched with calm approval, locking the shutter mechanism of the camera.

'What is happening?' Smolenko asked. 'This has gone far enough. You play with us.'

'Apparently our comrade doesn't feel like playing. But don't worry. He won't get away. Igor's covering the back entrance.'

Smolenko looked with a puzzled expression over the Saint's shoulder.

'Igor?'

Simon turned. Igor was standing there, beaming complacently.

'Igor covering *you*, comrade. Not so stupid as you think.'

'You pinheaded baboon—he's getting away!'

The Saint shoved the man aside and raced towards the back door.

'Halt!' Igor cried, going for his pistol.

Smolenko's hand darted towards the guard's wrist, but Simon had already halted. Molière was bouncing out of sight down the alley in an old Renault. The Saint turned on Igor.

'Get Ivan to help you, and catch that man. I don't care if it takes you the rest of your life . . . find Molière!'

'I demand to know what is going on,' Smolenko said.

'Okay, I'll show you. Watch.'

Simon brought out the lighter.

'You see, this has a delayed action adjustment on it. You can press the shutter release button and the shutter won't actually open for ten seconds. I'll set it on delayed action. I've taken nine pictures. This will be the tenth and last.'

He walked several yards along the alley to a waist-high garbage pail. Setting the delayed-action switch and pressing the shutter button, he dropped the miniature camera into the metal pail and came quickly away.

'Stay over here, now, and in just about three seconds...'

There was a loud, muffled boom, and the walls of the pail bulged fatly outward as the lid took off for housetop level. The Saint's and Smolenko's eyes, along with Igor's and Ivan's, followed the trajectory of the metal disc until it clattered back to the cobblestones of the alley.

'There but for the grace of God go I,' Simon said soberly.

'Igor,' Smolenko said, her eyes full of fire, her voice like a sabre blade slashing air, 'go and find that man.'

She slipped into Russian, but it was clear from her tone if nothing else that Comrade Molière could not look forward to a very happy life in the near future, and that that future might not be very extensive.

Smolenko confronted the Saint as Ivan and Igor pounded away on the double.

'Now,' she said. 'How do you know this?'

She jerked her head towards the bulging garbage can. Her voice was dangerous, but the Saint was not easily awed.

'I saw the device demonstrated in Berlin, by a gentleman working with Western intelligence: A lighter, exactly like that one, exploding on the tenth frame.'

'So,' she said, 'it *is* your people behind this.'

'No. They were merely trying to understand the workings of your equipment—the equipment, I mean, which has developed such a nasty habit of blowing up in your agents' faces of late. I already explained to you on the train about the British fear of pointless bloodshed among their agents and yours.'

'Very humane. And I am supposed to believe your stories?'

'How many times do I have to save your life before you begin to have a little faith in me?'

'Faith is stupidity.'

'I think it would also be slightly stupid to wait here until some cop who heard the explosion comes looking for what made it.'

She looked at him as he hurried her away from the music shop. When she finally spoke again, her voice was more subdued.

'I thank you. For saving my life.'

'I suppose you're welcome. I haven't decided yet.'

They continued on for several minutes through a tangle of back streets.

'I'll say one thing for you,' Simon remarked. 'You're probably the first woman I've ever met who can keep up with my pace when I'm evading the law.'

'I walk three miles every morning.'

'If you'd like to compete,' Simon said, 'we could try wrestling.'

Smolenko smiled, and it was the first time the Saint had seen in her expression the vestiges of the child which linger in the faces of most really beautiful women.

'I might injure you,' she said.

'I shudder to think what I might do to you.'

She looked away and slowed her steps as they passed the display window of a *parfumerie*.

'These goods are very expensive, I suppose,' she said with elaborate casualness.

'I'm surprised you'd notice.'

'Mr. Templar, your insinuations to the contrary, I am not quite a total automaton. I notice the colours of fabrics. I enjoy nice smells. If I were a man I should use shaving lotions, which are pleasant and effective. Since I am a woman I use perfume, on some suitable occasions, and I wear dresses and often stockings. I even have experienced a love life, it may astonish you to learn. We have no need of false inhibitions in the socialist state.'

'And you accept that some love life is necessary for the procreation of the race.'

'Of course, but...' She broke off abruptly. 'This is a ridiculous conversation. Are we going to the hotel by this route?'

'Eventually. For the moment we're probably safer wandering around here than sitting back at the hotel.'

'Safer?' she asked. 'But certainly Molière will not think of trying to harm us now that we know about him. He will be too busy trying to save himself.'

'Colonel, I'm surprised at you. Do you seriously think that Molière is the root of the problem, or even the most important part of it? He was much too easy a nut to crack. He gave himself away almost from the instant we walked into that shop. He was inept and practically shaking with fear when the scheme he'd been taking part in at a comfortable distance moved on to his own doorstep. He's only a piece in the puzzle.'

'Igor and Ivan will find him—and see that he talks.'

'Before that, he may talk to his own associates, and they will reorganize to have another go at us. Probably they have something in the works already, since they know they flunked out on the train. In the meantime, we may as well amuse ourselves. The shops will still be open for another couple of hours, and I need to do a little shopping. I didn't have time to pack a bag before I caught that train in Berlin.'

'We shall part here then,' Smolenko said.

'For safety's sake, let's meet at this spot in two hours and go back to the hotel together. Then I shall have the privilege, I hope, of taking the most beautiful colonel in the world out for one of the most beautiful dinners in the world. Assuming we don't get our heads blown off over cocktails.'

SIX

'THERE is no such company as Grossmeyer, Cardin et Fils,' said Simon, 'in Zurich or anywhere near it.'

They had just come back to the suite. The golden light of a setting sun fell directly through the windows, giving a touch of splendour to the otherwise uninspiring rooms.

'So that is why you went to the telegraph office and looked at the directories,' Smolenko said.

His blue eyes opened wide and mocking.

'Do you actually admit that you were following me?'

She smiled.

'Why, of course.'

'I somehow sensed those lovely brown eyes on the back of my neck,' Simon said calmly, 'but I figured you were safer toddling along after me than getting yourself lost in the big, bad city. Didn't I lose you right after the wineshop?'

'Yes, but I picked up your trail again as you came from the clothing store.'

'Which one? The men's or the women's?'

'The men's,' Smolenko said matter-of-factly. 'Why would you go to a store for women?'

She hesitated, momentarily flustered as he simply looked at her tolerantly.

'Of course,' she said. 'Presents for some friend. But that is not my affair. I am glad I discovered nothing that would make it necessary for me to consider you my enemy. I must admit that I am now inclined to trust you, for the present, and to believe that other elements must have somehow infiltrated my own organization.'

'Brilliant, Colonel. Better late than never. Incidentally, what *is* your name?'

'You know it.'

'Don't tell me you have only one. In Russian novels they always have five or six at the very least, and they get called something different on every page.'

She smiled, and again there was that reflection of inner warmth and irrepressible youth the Saint had noticed on the street that afternoon.

'It's Tanya,' she said. 'Very common. Very easy.'

She was standing by one of the tables, and Simon stepped towards her.

'But there's nothing common about you, *tovarishtch*,' he said softly.

She took a step backward, turned, and moved to the door of her room. For him the retreat was a form of flattery. If she had been uninterested—as women never seemed to be in a man so almost impossibly handsome as Simon Templar—she would most likely have stood her ground to freeze him off.

'I take a bath now,' she said. 'It is very warm here, after Moscow.'

'Please don't consider my bourgeois sensitivities, any time you feel like undressing accordingly. As you were saying...'

A knock at the door interrupted him, and in an instant his hand was on the lock.

'Who's there?' he asked.

'Packages for you, *m'sieu*.'

Simon's sensitive ears recognized the voice of one of the *chasseur*s who had brought them to the suite earlier in the day. The man came into the room, both arms supporting a heap of parcels retained by his chin. The Saint sorted through the pile as Tanya watched from the door of her room and the bellhop went happily away with his *pourboire*.

'You are most generous with my expense account,' Tanya said caustically.

'Don't talk like a capitalist, Comrade Colonel. I paid for these things personally.'

He turned towards her, holding a large flat box wrapped in white paper and tied with red ribbon.

'Here. A little something for you.'

For a presumably hard-boiled survivor of Soviet political shuffles, Colonel Smolenko blushed somewhat easily. She was openly astonished, and the Saint was a little touched that it should never even have occurred to her that his visit to the ladies' clothing shop could have been on her behalf.

'You must be wrong,' she said. 'Not for me.'

She was shaking her head even as she held out her hands to accept the box.

'I'm quite sure I'm not wrong,' Simon answered. 'Who'd know better than the one who picked it out?'

'Well, thank you,' she said quietly.

She put the package on a table next to her bedroom door, then looked at him as her hands touched the red bow. For an instant she brought herself to something like the military posture of attention.

'Thank you,' she repeated with great correctness.

'You're welcome. Open it please, if you will. One never knows when something is going to explode these days, and I'd just as soon get the suspense over with.'

She pulled the bow loose, apparently being careful to avoid any appearance of excited haste. Before she lifted the cardboard top she looked over at him, questioningly. He nodded. She peered inside.

'Oh, what beautiful . . .' she began.

She brought out a mass of shimmering pale satin and spread it on the bed.

'A lovely dress,' she whispered. 'And shoes. But what shoes.'

She held them up, and she was almost laughing. The slender heels were three inches high, and the tops were almost non-existent.

'*I?*' she said. 'Wear these?'

She studied Simon's face for a moment. Her expression became suspicious.

'You make fun of me?'

It was a suggestion rather than an accusation.

'Nothing could be farther from my mind,' the Saint said. 'Why would I throw away perfectly good and expensive clothes just for a laugh? There's more, too.'

'I see.'

But she didn't inspect the smaller black lacy items while he was watching.

'Thank you very much,' she said awkwardly, but with genuine feeling. 'Now I shall go wash and dress myself.'

As she was closing her door she looked back again.

'This is very good of you.'

Simon discovered, after finishing his own shaving, bathing, and changing, that female Soviet colonels are no more prompt in dressing for dinner than most other varieties of female. He called room service for ice and water, inspected the delivery for bombs and other quaint attachments, and poured himself a Peter Dawson. He was standing by the fireplace in his dinner jacket, meditating on the strange whims of whatever Fate it is that decides which lives shall cross, when Tanya came out of her room.

To say that he was overwhelmed at the sight of her would be to underestimate the Saint's capacity for subtleties of feeling. In addition to the normal elation produced by the close proximity of any exceptionally beautiful woman, he experienced a curious thrill at the thought that, Svengali-like, he was partly responsible for bringing the beauty into open bloom.

He bowed his respects, and Tanya smiled hesitantly. Her self-consciousness, like that of a girl going to her first formal dance, was as charming to an observer as it probably was uncomfortable for her. The brown hair which had been suppressed into a tight wad at the back of her head now fell free and soft around her face to her bare shoulders. Her face, though innocent of make-up except for lipstick, was lovely enough to have graced the cover of any Hollywood magazine—which struck Simon, who momentarily wished he had the time to arrange such a photographic appearance for her, as the perfect joke on both the magazine and the Soviet Secret Police.

'You're a gorgeous woman,' he said simply, and kissed her hands.

'You are very kind. I still do not understand...'

'Why I'd get you these things?'

'Yes.'

'I like giving presents, especially to attractive young ladies who're living in hotels in Paris with me. It's a weakness of mine.'

Tanya underwent another of her incongruous blushes.

'You embarrass me.'

Simon gave her a devilish look as he took the stole she carried and draped it expertly over her shoulders.

'Do I detect a trace of still unviolated bourgeois morality?' he asked.

'You may detect all kinds of strange things. I am suddenly like a fish out of water, in a world I never saw with my own two eyes before, and with a man I...'

Simon looked at her expectantly without interrupting as she paused. Suddenly the old suspicious shadow fell across her face again.

'You think I come here without clothes to wear in the Paris restaurants?'

The Saint took her arm and pressed her hand.

'Tanya, don't you have any proverb in Russian about gift horses? When I give intimate gifts such as dresses or lacy lingerie to a lady, it's not because I think she has nothing else to wear. I promise you, my motives weren't in the least noble or charitable.'

'Well, you would have been right,' she admitted with a sheepish little smile. 'I did not have anything proper to wear.'

The telephone rang, and the Saint answered it. He recognized Ivan's thick voice in the receiver.

'*Dascha*,' Ivan said tersely.

'I beg your pardon?'

'*Dascha*,' the MGB man repeated impatiently. 'Say her *dascha*.'

Simon covered the mouthpiece with his hand and turned to Tanya.

'It's Ivan. He wants me to say you "*dascha*", whatever that means.'

'My code name,' she explained, taking the phone. 'You don't expect him to ask for Colonel Smolenko.'

She engaged in some heated Russian interchange which seemed to grow increasingly angry on her part and sparse on Ivan's. She clamped down the receiver as if hitting the table with her fist.

'Idiots. They traced Molière to a village twenty kilometres from Paris but have not found him yet.'

'Where's Ivan now?'

'A café in some place called Villeneuve, south of here. They are trying to hire a car. They promise they find Molière by morning. They assure me that they have his location, how do you say it, pinned down? But they will not be back here tonight.'

'Well, that's very good. I don't think we need them. With the local boss—who I assume is Molière—on the run it should take the Ungodly at least until tomorrow to conjure up another blast. Let's see Paris, shall we?'

They did not see all of Paris, but they saw some of the best that Simon knew, which was the best there was. After cocktails in the jam-packed sophistication of the George V, he took her to dinner at the Tour d'Argent, not perhaps so much for its famous *canard à la presse* as for the entrancing view over the Seine to the floodlit cathedral of Notre Dame. Then when they were full of rich food and beauty and a bottle of '34 Cheval Blanc settled with *ballons* of Delamain cognac, the intimacy of a short taxi ride transported them with hardly a perceptible break to one of those impeccably discreet hideaways which still defy the rising din of the discothèques, for those who prefer the Old World trappings of romance, a place of candlelight, soft music for dancing, and an agreeable absence of tourists.

After a few glasses of champagne on top of their earlier libations, Tanya Smolenko was as off guard and mildly giggly as most other women would have been under similar circumstances. The Saint led her on to the minuscule dance floor, whose meagre dimensions were designed to foster intimate contact rather than terpsichorean athletics, and took her in his arms.

'I must admit,' he said, 'that this is one of the most peculiar experiences of my life.'

Their bodies swayed slowly together to the muted sounds of gypsy violins.

'Bizarre,' she said, 'but very nice.'

'There's no other place like Paris, really.'

'All cities look well at night.'

'Tanya,' he said, 'why don't you relax and enjoy it? Answer me truthfully: doesn't all this make your heart beat just the tiniest bit faster?'

'My heart? Of course not. What does it have to do with my heart?'

'You must have a heart somewhere.'

He slipped his right hand around and under her breast for a moment.

'There,' he said, 'you do have one. And you aren't telling me the truth. I estimate it's about twenty beats a minute above normal.'

'My heart rate is always high. It is my metabolism. It has nothing to do with Paris.'

'No? How flattering. Anyway, it's a beautiful metabolism.'

He drew her closer to him, their eyes meeting in a wordless communication. Then his lips touched hers in a light leisurely way until she turned her head.

When they returned to the hotel, the trucks of fresh vegetables were rumbling through the city towards pre-dawn market, and the streets were wet from their nocturnal washing. It was one of those late hours which are best left indefinite, so as not to evoke exhaustion the next day by their very recollection.

Simon simply avoided looking at his watch, prolonging the blissful timeless state in which he and Tanya had existed since the sun went down. And if he, who had known virtually all the pleasures of the world, was happy, Tanya, who apparently had known very little beyond the comparatively harsh environment of her birthplace, was euphoric. She was also slightly drunk, which the Saint was not.

As they entered the suite and Simon closed the door, she held both his hands and looked him in the face.

'I had a most beautiful time.'

'So did I, Tanya; I think you'd make any night a success—when you were off duty.'

She smiled and slipped her hands to his shoulders, shyly inviting another kiss. But the Saint, moving closer, noticed something on the floor.

'I'm sorry,' he said, stooping to pick up the envelope, 'but these days one can't be too careful. It's for you, my dear. Feels light and flexible enough. Probably the only thing explosive involved will be me if it turns out to be a billet-doux from a rival admirer.'

She smiled and looked curiously at the envelope.

'From Switzerland.'

'Do all women do that?' Simon asked, going over to the fresh bucket of ice and bottle of Evian he'd requested in advance be sent up to keep his bottle of Peter Dawson company after the witching hour.

'What?'

'Try to figure out who letters are from before they open them. Don't you have agents in Switzerland?'

She was intent now on slitting the envelope and unfolding the rather heavy paper of the letter. Simon, in order not to seem to pry, devoted his attention to pouring drinks. Tanya's scream took him by surprise.

'Simon! What...'

He saw the edges of the letter, as if touched by an invisible flame, begin to curl and turn brown.

'Drop it!' he snapped, and reacted faster than a pouncing cat.

By the time the letter reached the floor he was emptying the ice and water from the bucket over it. His aim was so accurate that the paper was completely sodden, and after emitting a few dying wisps of steam it lay harmlessly on the carpet, a wrinkled sheet of scorched brown.

'The envelope,' Tanya said.

Simon had already thought of that and assured himself that it lay inert and inactive where Tanya had let it fall.

'Your friends,' he said, 'impress me with the variety of distractions they manage to throw our way. I don't know if that was supposed to burn us up, blow us up, or gas us, but...'

'When I find who does this...'

'You and me both,' Simon said, admiring the expressively murderous clenching of her fist.

'I crush him like a bedbug.'

'I've never had the pleasure of that particular type of violence, but I sympathize completely with your feelings.'

He picked up the envelope and examined it.

'Lined with black inside. Sealed airtight, I'm sure. The paper was obviously some sort of plastic sensitized to go off when it was exposed to light and air.'

Tanya stood directly in front of him and looked into his eyes very seriously.

'Simon Templar, I have come to trust you. For good reasons. This is the third time, at least, that you save my life. And I know that being together like this, and being who we are, we ... have a physical attraction. But that could happen even between enemies. A biological thing. I am not ashamed of it.'

'Neither am I.'

'But Simon—who am I to think ... After all, consider my position. Who am I to think is behind these things if not the British and Americans? Surely not my own men.

Why? Why would they? The whole thing is so pointless. For instance I carry no information or plans in my head on this mission which would make me dangerous to any nation. There is nothing I might reveal. And if I were gone, somebody else would immediately replace me. Yet there have been several attempts on my life already. Can you blame me for suspecting the most obvious enemy?'

'No,' Simon said quietly. 'It seems to me there are several possibilities, at least. One, that I'm lying, and I'm really here as a hostile agent—but the silliness of that should be pretty obvious by now. I've certainly shown I don't want you dead. A second possibility is of some kind of upheaval or take-over plot within your own organization, but . . .'

'I have thought of that many times, of course. But it makes no sense, and I have checked every facet. There is no pattern to the killing, to who is killed.'

'You'd know about that much better than I. Incidentally, I assume that not all these spying devices of yours are booby-trapped. Just one here and one there, enough to do the job without tipping you off as to the cause. You obviously didn't know it was their own little gadgets that were blowing up your agents until I told you.'

She nodded, too preoccupied to bother defending herself.

'But you see the advantage to the British, for example,' she said. 'So no one of the agents killed is especially important . . . but the constant fear of our equipment exploding would bring about a serious cut-back in our activities. We would be forced to recall every piece of apparatus.'

'That makes perfect sense,' said the Saint. 'All I can do is say again that to the best of my knowledge our side is as concerned about this as you are. The fact that I'm here with you should be some kind of evidence of that. And another thing: It seems to me that any kind of cutback you'd be forced to make because of these bombs would be so temporary it wouldn't do us an ounce of good. I think you've got to count that out.'

'What do we count in, then?' asked Smolenko.

'One remote possibility would be some individual joker who gets a private kick out of disintegrating Russian agents, but I don't think any one nut could possibly handle this operation, and the chances of several nuts sharing the same mania and working together are practically infinitesimal. We have to look somewhere else for the answer.'

'Where?'

'You must have thought of it yourself,' he said.

'Of course. China. But it seems so much less likely than ...'

'Seemed, I hope,' said Simon. 'I thought I was beginning to convince you.'

She smiled and seemed to become a woman again after her reversion to official capacity. She squeezed his hand and kissed him on the cheek.

'I am afraid it is all too easy now for you to convince me of anything. Especially because I've had so much to drink.'

She drew back a little, still smiling.

'But let me ask you one thing,' she continued. 'Would it not be rather clever of the British or Americans or whoever to make me *think* it is the Chinese behind this—and in that way putting a bigger split between us and another socialist power?'

'It would be very clever, Tanya,' the Saint said, touching the end of her nose with one finger, 'but not half as clever as you. You're as sharp as a needle even when you're tipsy. I think the only way we'll ever convince you—and me—is to go right to the source of the whole thing.'

'Simon, you are not so smart. If we knew the source we would have no problem.'

'Tanya, when you have only fragments to work with, little things become significant. You remember where Molière said the miniaturized equipment comes from?'

'Zurich.'

'Zurich. From Grossmeyer, etc. But of course there is no Grossmeyer. And yet when we were still at that record shop I noticed shipping cartons marked Grossmeyer, Cardin, and so forth, mailed from Altbergen—Altbergen being a tiny village in the mountains in south-east Switzerland.'

He turned to her from the pacing he'd begun.

'Now, do you know how I know about this obscure village of Altbergen, which would hardly be found on anything but a local hiker's map?'

'Because you have hiked there?'

'No, Altbergen is one spot I've never been to. But I've heard of it, and this afternoon I was reminded of it by more than the packing cartons. You remember the bottle of liqueur, Grand Abrouillac, that Molière was so kind as to offer us this afternoon?'

'It seems like years ago.'

'Your mind is wandering, sweetheart. You do remember?'

'Of course.'

'Well, Grand Abrouillac is made in only one place in the world—a monastery in Altbergen, Switzerland.'

'Simon, that's fine, but it still does not mean that we know . . .'

'Take another look at this, please.'

He handed her the envelope in which the incendiary paper had been mailed.

'The postmark,' she said. 'Altbergen.'

She looked at the envelope more closely, and then at him.

'So,' said Simon with the satisfaction that comes of seeing order emerge from chaos, 'I think that if Igor and Ivan haven't come up with Molière and plenty of facts by early morning, you and I should take off for Switzerland.'

'Alone?'

'Don't shatter all my new illusions, Tanya. You mean you still believe in bourgeois institutions like chaperones? Or don't you think I'm as good a bodyguard as Ivan or Igor?'

He had poured drinks for both of them, and he put hers in a passive hand.

'Of course, I can leave orders for them to follow us; if we are not here, they will know where to ask for instructions.'

'You aren't afraid of shocking them?' he mocked her. 'You were on a trip with them when I met you, but I didn't assume they were your lovers. Would such good Soviet Boy Scouts have naughtier minds than mine?'

They were standing close together, and as Tanya sipped her drink her lips moved charmingly into a smile.

'I do not know what is in your mind,' she said, 'but if you wish to be my lover I expect you to ask me. In such things men should take the lead.'

SEVEN

Simon had called the concierge for a mid-morning flight to Zurich, and just before noon the plane bearing him and Tanya set down at the Zurich airfield. He had arranged in advance for a U-drive car to be waiting, and in a matter of minutes they were on their way into the town, and then driving on through it and out again along the north shore of the lake.

'We'll have lunch at the Ermitage at Kusnacht—it's just a few miles farther on,' he said. 'There's a beautiful shady terrace right on the water, and their *filets de perche à la mode du fils du pêcheur* are something that has to be tasted to be believed.'

The setting and the meal were as perfect as he had promised, and perfectly accompanied by the bottle of ice-cold dry Aigle of Montmollin which he ordered.

'I think you are the most decadent man I have ever personally met,' she remarked thoughtfully.

He grinned with Saintly impudence.

'And aren't you loving it?'

'We have work to do, and all you think of is what we should eat and drink.'

'For tomorrow we die—maybe. And that's not *all* I think of, as you ought to remember.' He held her eyes until she lowered them. 'Besides, I've never found I could work better for missing a good meal.'

'And while you are enjoying all this, do you never think of the millions in the world who are starving?'

'Sometimes. But I can't convince myself that if I wasn't eating it, any of them would get it.'

'You are impossible,' she said, and he laughed.

'What did you expect of a horrible capitalist?'

Nevertheless, no one who had been observing them would have taken them for enemies when they left to drive on towards the mountains just faintly visible in the distance.

From the air the Alps had appeared like a great wall of cloud near the horizon, but after Simon and Tanya crossed the lake and bore away to the south-east the peaks took on their true forms as the car began to climb twisting and steeper roads. The winter snows, now just a fading memory in Paris and even in Zurich, stubbornly clung on even below the timber line, where later in the summer, when the whiteness had withdrawn further, the last venturesome scraggly firs would be seen manning the frontier between the rich verdure of the forests below and the raw grey expanses of stone above.

Altbergen was the kind of place whose existence is announced to the traveller by a minute sign pointing from the highway up something like a glorified cow path. Though Simon had found it on the map, he almost passed the turning, but managed to get his brakes down in time to make the sudden transition from modern highway engineering to rural improvisation.

The car bounded from boulder to pothole with protesting rattles, and it became increasingly obvious as the angle of climb approached something like fifty degrees that what they were on was possibly not a cow path at all, but an occasional river bed gouged out by the torrents of thawing spring.

Luckily for the automobile, as well as its occupants, the distance from highway to Altbergen was only seven kilometres—straight up, it seemed at times. But the drive was invigorating, shaking out any last traces of sluggishness traceable to the previous long and perhaps over-indulgent evening.

Altbergen was as surprised to see Tanya and Simon as Tanya and Simon were relieved to see it. Set on the green slope of a tiny plateau, its site constituted the only place within miles where more than three houses together might have clung to the ground. As it was, there were not many buildings, perhaps twenty, including a small inn and a few starkly essential shops.

'It's beautiful,' Tanya said. 'I have seen it only in picture books. Like gingerbread houses.'

'Anyway,' Simon remarked, 'if Ivan and Igor get this far, they won't have much of a search to locate us.'

He parked in front of the inn, joining company with a pair of Volkswagens and a squarish *deux chevaux* whose natural tendency to look like a corrugated tin lean-to had apparently been well assisted by numerous trips between Altbergen and the nearest paved road. From across the narrow street, the combined grocer and hardware merchant peered through his display window at the Zurich licence plate. The servant girl who had been sweeping the threshold of the *Gasthof* with no great enthusiasm in the first place came to a complete halt as she gaped curiously at the novelty of city tourists—and rich ones, too, by the looks of them—coming to the Goldener Hirsch and unloading baggage with the apparent intention of making a stay.

Altbergen's isolation from the conveniences of modern life meant that checking in simply consisted of being led up the steep stairs by the plump proprietress while the servant girl, a slim blonde creature, staggered along behind with all the luggage, refusing Simon's offers of help. There was no surrender of passports for inspection by the police overnight, no filling out of lengthy forms in the usual European manner, whereby one gains entry to sleeping quarters only by confessing in detail a large part of one's own and one's relatives' pasts, and explaining precisely whence one has come and where one is going. There was not even a register to sign, and the proprietress had not asked for names.

'*So, bitte,*' she said, smiling as she opened the door of what was obviously the best room, '*schön, nicht wahr?*'

'*Sehr schön,*' Simon agreed, before Tanya could make any other comment.

The walls were all natural wood, with the lingering smell of fresh-cut lumber about them. There were two beds, huge and solid, with white comforters a foot thick but light as air. Beyond the double doors was an ornate balcony of the kind that fronted the upper floors of almost every house in the village.

'I didn't want to attract more attention by asking for separate rooms,' Simon explained innocently to Tanya, in English. He went on more wickedly: 'The only problem will be if Ivan and Igor get here. Which of them would you rather double up with?'

She turned away quickly, towards the balcony.

'Supper is from six o'clock,' the proprietress said in leaving. 'If you want hot water or anything, the bell is there.'

'Oh, Simon, come look.'

Tanya was outside, deeply breathing the sharp clear air. The view she wanted him to see was superb: the snow-covered Alps, the dark green meadows studded with outcroppings of pale stone, the shingled roofs of the houses weighted with chunks of the same rock. There was a peace and timelessness totally unlike any other in the world.

He turned from the view to her, and thought that she looked happier than he had ever seen her. There had been very good moments, but the kind of deep-down contentment that he sensed in her now was something new and different. They seemed a long long way from subterfuge, treachery, and murder.

'You like it here?' he asked her.

'Very much. Yes.'

'There's a great feeling of freedom, isn't there?'

She nodded, smiling at the world in general.

'Perhaps.'

'More than you could ever have in Russia?' the Saint said.

Such a challenge had been on his mind for some time, but he had hesitated again and again to put it to her for fear she would assume that his true mission all along had been to tempt her to defect from the communist world. But if ever there was to be a moment to risk disrupting the rapport they had begun to achieve, this might have been it.

He realized his misjudgement instantly, in a silence that could almost be physically felt.

'I'm sorry,' he said after a moment. 'That wasn't very subtle ... I suppose in your position, especially if one has relatives, even close friends who might ... face some unpleasant consequences, it makes it difficult even to think about.'

She stood straighter, slipping her elbows from the broad rail of the balcony.

'I have never thought in such a way. It is not only difficult, it is impossible.'

'Then why are you so touchy about it?' he asked gently.

'I should be. You are hinting at treason, not talking about a ... a trip to the seaside.'

He put his hands soothingly on her shoulders.

'All right. We'll let it pass, okay? This is no time or place to start arguing ideologies. We both have a job to do.'

He could feel the tension begin to fade from her body. She took her lower lip between her teeth for a moment and looked him in the face before she answered.

'Okay,' she said, and she had to start smiling again just because she'd used that American expression.

'See up there?' the Saint said, pointing. 'That looks as if it could be the monastery.'

'Where they make the liqueur.'

'Mm-hm. And somewhere around here somebody's making something else—and I don't mean that stew and red cabbage you smell.'

'Booby traps, I think you call them.'

'Yes. Well put. Now you can unpack and freshen up and prepare to greet me properly upon my heroic return.'

'Where are you going?'

'Trap shooting, of course.'

She followed him back into the bedroom.

'I go with you.'

He hesitated for a moment, and shrugged.

'Okay, if you like. This is your affair as much as mine. We shouldn't run into anything on the first reconnaissance where you'd be a liability.'

'Really! You forget who I am. In the Soviet Union we recognize no difference between the sexes.'

'Well, I do,' said Simon, 'but then I've had my memory refreshed recently.'

'That was not what I meant. My English . . .'

'Your English is fine, and so are you. Now let's get going so we can be back here in time for that supper. I have the distinct impression that if we don't dine here we don't dine anywhere, unless you're up to a few unrolled oats from some farmer's horse trough.'

They went downstairs and accosted the servant girl, who was still reluctantly applying her broomstraws to the smoothly worn wood of the entranceway, and Simon asked her if there were any factories in the area. He might have asked for dinosaurs.

'Factories, sir? Like where they make autos and things?'

'Any kind of factories.'

The girl shook her head.

'No. The only thing we make here is cheese, and there is no factory for that. It is done by the farmers at home.'

'Well,' Simon said, 'in that case, thank you very much.'

'*Bitte sehr*. If you wish to see a factory you must go down to Zurich.'

Tanya turned back as she and Simon started away.

'I have a small radio that does not work. Can someone here fix it?'

'*Nein. Es tut mir leid*. We have no one to fix anything. If you want things like that, why do you come here?'

'Because I really love peace and quiet,' said the Saint.

He set a course that took them through the inquisitive village, across a little stream covered by a neatly built wooden bridge, and along a path that led straight up the slope of the surrounding meadow.

Tanya looked up ahead of them to the spot on the mountainside where man-made walls of grey stone were half hidden by evergreens.

'I hope you are not taking me on a wild-goose hunt,' she said, avoiding one of the manifold traces which grazing cows had left behind.

'"Chase",' Simon corrected her. 'I didn't really expect to find a transistor radio factory bringing prosperity to the peasants up here at the end of nowhere, but there just has to be some link with it.'

'At the monastery?'

'Yes. Think you can make it?'

'Of course. I can still be walking after you have dropped on your face.'

But she underestimated both the distance and Simon's hard-muscled health. His sense of direction took them briskly on across the remainder of the Alpine meadow, past lovely patches of blue and yellow wild flowers, to the foot of a rocky trail that led through the dense forest that clung to the mountainside. A rustic sign with lettering carved precisely into it said: KLOSTER ¾ St.

'Three-quarters of an hour from here,' he said. 'But if you're in such great shape, we should be able to shave that to a half.'

He set off at a pace that would not have disgraced an energetic chamois. The slope was soon so steep that the path, such as it was, had to zigzag back and forth to maintain a reasonable gradient. Simon went on with springy steps, smiling to himself as he sensed Tanya's increasing difficulties. He took a makeshift staff from some branches left by woodcutters and began to sing cheerily as they climbed on.

> *'Mein Vater war ein Wandersmann*
> *Und ich hab's auch im Blut,*
> *Ich wandere hin, ich wandere her,*
> *Und habe frischen Mut.*
> *Valeri, valera,*
> *Valeri, valera-ha-ha-ha-ha-ha*
> *Valeri, valera,*
> *Und schwenke meinen Hut.'*

'Stop!' she cried at last; and he stopped and turned, with raised eyebrows.

'Am I that bad? It's an old Tirolean song—perfectly respectable. I thought it went well with the scenery.'

'I can't go on . . . so fast,' she panted shamelessly.

'Must be the thin air at this altitude,' Simon said, with devastating concern. 'I should have remembered—it can get the greatest athletes down at first.'

She called him something unkind in Russian and flopped down on a pile of cut wood to rest.

'It can't be much further now,' he said, after giving her a minute to catch her breath. 'When we get there, just don't say anything till I've decided what line to take.'

'Don't you know what you are going to say?'

He shrugged.

'Only vaguely. It depends on what reception we get. But I have great faith in my ability to improvise. It hasn't failed me yet.'

They came again to the stream they had crossed down in the meadow; here it had its source, gushing like a miraculous fountain from the rocks. Then, almost without warning, the cold stone of the monastery rose in front of the Saint and Smolenko. Whatever was inside the encircling walls could not be seen from where Simon and Tanya stood. Gates of massive hardwood braced with handwrought iron were solidly closed, and the only means of communication with the inside appeared to be a rusty bell with a pull-rope of plaited cowhide.

'Shall we?'

The Saint rang the bell, and for a long time there was no sound but the twittering of birds and the whisper of an afternoon breeze in the pine needles. Then, like something entirely unearthly, the voices of melodiously chanting men came from within the walls.

'They sound like professionals,' Simon said.

Tanya gave him a wry look.

'They are, of course,' she said. 'Professional parasites on superstitious ignorance.'

'Oh, dear comrade, let's not go into that.'

He rang again, vigorously, hoping to make the bell heard over the monkly devotions.

'It might be more polite to wait till they've finished, but they're liable to go on for hours,' he explained. 'From what little I know about this order, they're extremely hard on themselves. Don't show their faces or say anything except prayers, except for one brother who has a dispensation to conduct any essential business. Dig their own graves and sleep in coffins and scourge themselves twice a day.'

'Charming,' said Tanya.

There was a rattling sound inside the thick gate, and a sliding board about a foot long and six inches high slid back to show a cowled and black-veiled head. The head said nothing, just hovered there.

'*Gruss Gott*,' said the Saint. 'May we come in?'

The monk pressed his eyes to the opening as if to see whether or not there were others in the party.

'*Gruss Gott*,' the head replied in a voice much less sepulchral than its visible source. 'There is not much to see.'

'I was told that visitors were always welcome if they made a contribution,' Simon said mendaciously.

'The contribution is always twenty francs. For only two, that would be ten francs each.'

'I should be glad to give it to such a deserving order.'

The open panel slammed shut. There were clanking noises on the other side of the portals, and a moment later one of them creaked partially open. The monk stood with his hand silently extended, palm upwards, until Simon placed the requisite coins in it.

'I am Brother Anton. The Brotherhood are at their

devotions in the chapel, as you hear. It will be several hours before they come out, and of course I cannot allow you to disturb their meditations by entering that part of the building. But I will show you what little else I can.'

He gestured for them to follow, and together they crossed the open courtyard, which had a stone well with bucket and pulley in the centre, and small but profusely growing vegetable gardens around the sides.

The cloister was built of stone so old that its surface was pitted and often crumbling. Here and there an Alpine flower had found a home in some niche or crevice, and velvety green moss grew on the roof shingles. As Simon saw, led and lectured by Brother Anton, the place was in the shape of a square, with the chapel and library comprising one side, the monks' cells two sides, and the refectory and kitchen the fourth side. In the centre, by the well, was a small inner quadrangle quartered by crossing walkways and possessed of two stone benches and a stagnant birdbath.

Simon and Tanya were allowed a brief look at all areas except the chapel, from which continued to come the sound of harmoniously chanting male voices. In the kitchen a lone monk, cowled and veiled, stood watch over a gigantic pot on the wood-burning stove. He turned to look at the visitors without noticeable reaction and then went back to his cooking. From the pot came a familiar but somehow inappropriate aroma which Simon could not immediately pin down. His mind was busy with other things.

One of the attributes of a supremely alert intelligence such as the Saint's is the ability to see the relationship between apparently unrelated facts. As he listened politely to Brother Anton's historical notes and pretended to study the architectural details of the ancient building, his thoughts were hours ahead. He was noticing the interesting but seemingly irrelevant fact that the pump in the kitchen, the well in the courtyard, and the source of the stream outside the walls were in a more or less direct line.

'And so,' Brother Anton was concluding, 'for five centuries, for those who joined us here, the world ended at that door through which you entered.'

'But one worldly thing still comes out through it,' Simon said, 'but for which we might never have heard of this place. Is it possible to see the manufacture of Grand Abrouillac?'

He was curious to know whether the cenobite was frowning or smiling under his veil in response to that additional request.

'To see the place, but not to see the method,' was the reply. 'Therefore, to see very little. But come this way.'

'We must not stay long,' Simon said pointedly, looking at his watch. 'We have friends below in the village who will come up looking for us if we do not return for supper. I don't want them to start worrying about us.'

'It will take only a minute to see what I am permitted to show,' the monk said.

He led the way down stone steps made smoothly concave by scores of years of sandalled treading. Now they were in a basement whose only windows were narrow grated slits near the ceiling at the level of the ground outside. The walls were lined with the spiralled bottles such as Simon had seen in Molière's office. Jars of herbs and unidentifiable liquids gathered dust on other shelves. Pungently spirituous casks and vats stood about the floor and were racked in tiers along one wall. There was a big wood-burning stove at one end of the room with a flue extending into the ceiling.

'Central heat?' Simon inquired.

'Yes. It becomes very cold here even in summer. Only a

few hundred metres above us is always snow.'

'No point in mortifying the flesh that much,' Simon commented in English.

'*Bitte?*'

'I suppose it would be bad for the brew to freeze.'

The Saint touched a kind of thick wooden tap in the wall, from behind which came a faint gurgling sound.

'The mountain spring water which is one of the secret ingredients?'

'*Sie haben recht.* The water is most important.'

The monk took a bottle from one of the shelves.

'If you wish to take a bottle with you, it is forty francs here, much less than outside.'

Simon took a note from his pocket and pressed it into the man's hand.

'*Danke sehr, Bruder.* For your holy work.'

'*Vielen Dank.*'

'*Bitte.*'

As they started up the stairs, Simon indicated a large ceiling fan which had been almost invisible from directly below because of a kind of false ceiling hung under it.

'You have installed some other modern comforts, I see.'

'*Ach, ja.* The fumes, you know. In the old days the brothers used to become quite drunk while working here, merely from breathing.'

'All good things must come to an end, I suppose.'

'All good things and all bad things,' the monk said, and quickly showed them the way out of the cloisters to the main doorway.

Simon had gone with Tanya only a few yards out of sight of the walls when he took her arm and said: 'Excuse me just a moment.'

He knelt down and put the bottle of Grand Abrouillac between two rocks and covered it with pine needles.

'As much as I love good liquor, I love life more, and I'm in no mood to be poisoned, exploded, or shot in the head.'

She stared.

'You do not think...'

'I do think. And I wouldn't take any chances with anything that came out of that crypt. Now let's go on and make plenty of noise as we recede into the sunset.'

Twenty seconds later he stopped again. From above drifted the singing voices of the Brotherhood.

'Why do we wait?' Tanya whispered.

'To listen. I'm a student of bird calls and other forest noises.'

The vigil produced results more practical than aesthetic. After about two minutes the voices of the choristers stopped abruptly in mid-syllable, even in mid-note, to say nothing of mid-phrase.

The Saint and Tanya looked at one another.

'No wonder our friends sounded so professional,' Simon said. 'They were.'

'A gramophone record.'

'Right, my dear. The invisible Brotherhood is just about as genuine as everything else in that joint. Did you notice those vegetable plots? Weeds bigger than the cabbages. Nobody's bothered to cultivate them for days—or weeks.'

He took Tanya's hand, and they went on down the path.

'So,' she said, 'you think they make our equipment there?'

'Seems very likely. There could be all sorts of hidden chambers. I was studying that possibility, too, but we can't be sure until tonight.'

'Tonight?'

'Tonight. When I come back for another look around.

I've never liked these conducted tours. By the way,' he added with a quizzical frown, 'what do you think that was they were cooking in the kitchen?'

'I don't know,' she answered absently. 'Kasha? Rice?'

Suddenly Simon stopped and looked at her.

'Rice,' he said, and threw back his head and laughed.

EIGHT

A HALF-MOON was just riding high enough to illuminate the snow on the great peaks above as the Saint began his return climb to the monastery. Everything was silvered, the sky was clear, and the air was keener than it had been in the daytime. The cold wind's stimulus to his walking speed helped to nullify the reductive effect of his dinner (there was no menu and no choice) of goulash, noodles, and red cabbage.

Tanya had wanted to come, but he had convinced her that it was foolhardy for them both to be committed at the same time. If he had not returned by midnight she would be free to take whatever action she thought best—an old tactic but, like most lasting traditions, a sound one. It was almost ten o'clock now.

There was another logical reason for her to wait at the *Gasthof*: Igor and Ivan might arrive at any moment, following directions that had been left in Paris, and any news they had of Molière might be vital. Someone should be at the inn to meet them if they did turn up.

As he came closer to the monastery, Simon's stride slackened and became more stealthy, until the last yards were covered with the silence of a stalking cat. The silence within seemed to be just as complete, and the few leaded windows high up in the walls were dark, but he could not believe that all the inmates would go to sleep at the same time, leaving no one on watch, if his suspicions had any foundation.

He picked up a couple of pebbles in one hand, and stood with his back pressed against the wall to one side of the great doors. In his other hand he held the long branch which he had discarded there on his earlier visit. He reached over and tapped with it on the door. After a pause, he tapped again, insistently. And again.

He heard the spy-slot open, but knew he could not be seen from where he stood. He waited another second or two, and then scratched hard with his stick on the lower part of the far door, where the watcher inside would not possibly see what was doing it.

The panel slid shut, and bolts and bars scraped on the inside. The door gave a faint cautious creak, and the profile of a man came through the opening. But the man was no monk—at least, no monk in the regular accoutrements. He was wearing military style fatigues, boots, and a forage cap. Even more unorthodox was the large pistol he carried, its barrel lengthened by the thick cylinder of a silencer.

Before the sentry's widening arc of survey could swing around far enough to find him, Simon lobbed one of his pebbles straight ahead. The sound of its landing in the underbush opposite riveted the guard's eyes in that direction; the second pebble, tossed the same way, brought the man a step outside the door, his pistol at the ready.

It was as much space as the Saint needed. He stepped across in one long stride, swinging his stick numbingly into the watchman's larynx, and then bringing him down with one swift karate chop to the back of the neck.

Simon picked up the pistol and checked it quickly. As an afterthought, he also took the guard's forage cap and put it on—if any others should see him before he saw them, it might in near-darkness be just enough to disguise him for a few seconds that could make vital differences. Then he stepped in through the great doorway and pushed the door shut behind him until it just touched its mate without latching.

The courtyard was dark and deserted, but not all the windows that opened on to the interior were blacked out. The Saint moved on tiptoe towards the nearest one, which he recalled as belonging to the refectory. As soon as he was close enough to look in, he had complete and startling confirmation of what had only been a vague impression when he had glimpsed the doorkeeper's features in the moonlight.

The sight would undoubtedly have caused the founding father of Kloster Altbergen to sit up in his do-it-yourself grave and demand an entire keg of Grand Abrouillac, for his venerable dining hall was populated by half a dozen Chinese.

They were not dressed in grim woolly habits, but in shirt sleeves or white laboratory coats. They were not engaged in silent meditation, but in gambling games, idle conversation, and cigarette smoking.

On the whole they were not husky or even particularly robust-looking men, which led the Saint to the swift conclusion that they constituted a technical rather than a military task force. If there were other trained soldiers such as the guard probably had been, they were not in sight. And it also appeared that unless egalitarianism in China had gone further than he suspected, there appeared to be no leader among the group. The men had the air of comrades glad to be relaxing at the end of a day's routine work.

The Saint dragged himself away from that fascinating spectacle and moved around the cloisters until he came to another lighted window.

There he hit the jackpot: a rather overweight Chinese gentleman in a green uniform without insignia was sitting at a table in the library; with him was another man, not

Chinese but some variety of European. What language they were speaking could not be heard through the sealed glass. Between them on the table was a pile of gold coins and a sort of record book in which the Chinese—whom Simon immediately christened 'the general'—would occasionally write something.

The European, who the Saint now assumed to be 'Brother Anton', was not in black robes either, but in a suède jacket, and he seemed to have just concluded a discussion with the general. He stood and left the room as the Chinese went back to his calculations.

Simon flattened himself behind a pillar; Anton emerged through a narrow passage into the courtyard a few feet away. The erstwhile monk stretched his arms, took a deep breath, and admired the moon.

Then, as his gaze returned earthwards, he seemed to be transfixed by some much less pacifying vision. For three or four seconds he stood frozen in unnatural rigidity, and then he whirled around and rushed back to the entrance from which he had emerged, yelling something shrill and incomprehensible, but the Saint had no need of a literal translation to recognize the strident urgency of the alarm.

Looking around to discover what could have triggered it, he saw that the big door which he had been so careful to almost close was now wide open. The mild force of the wind could not possibly have moved the heavy gate on its hinges, and the guard Simon had disposed of would be out for some time more, if not permanently.

Turning back again the other way, the Saint had a glimpse through the window of the general scraping gold coins into a leather purse which he jammed in his pocket as he jumped to his feet. Anton lunged into the room and pressed a button which set off muted alarm bells throughout the monastery.

Simon stooped low and dashed for the well. Sticking the guard's automatic into his belt, he swung his legs over the waist-high circular wall, seized the doubled rope which hung from the pulley on the scaffolding above his head, and slid down so that he was just able to see what was happening around him.

He had already been asking himself if Tanya had followed alone, or if Ivan and Igor had arrived after he left and come up to the monastery with her. Then, as the Chinese were hurrying out of the refectory, he saw a shadowy figure dart from near the gate into the passage taken a few moments before by Anton.

He was sure it was Tanya. She had probably seen him in his borrowed cap and mistaken him for a guard. Seconds later he saw her through the lighted window holding a pistol on the general and Anton.

The alarm had roused the refectory, and an influx of shouting, confusedly milling people into the courtyard allowed the Saint no more time to watch Tanya's progress. He slipped down about two feet, straddled the bucket which swung at one end of the rope, and held himself steady by grasping the other strand. Knocking the forage cap deliberately from his head, he heard it plop into water just a couple of yards underneath him, and then he listened closely in order to follow the events taking place above.

An authoritative voice was calling out in Chinese over the hubbub, and all activity seemed to come to an abrupt halt. The excited shouts died away, and the running feet were still. Simon raised himself so that he could see. The half-dozen civilians, joined by Anton and a pair of men in uniforms like that of the guard who had originally been at the gate, were standing frozen, watching Tanya holding her pistol near the general's head in one of the archways.

She and her hostage had apparently already discovered

that they had a common language in English.

'Tell them to be still and put their guns down, or I shoot you,' she said. 'Also, my men are watching and will fire if they resist.'

'Yes,' said the general.

He called something in Chinese, and the guards dropped their weapons.

'Where is that pig, Templar?' Tanya asked.

The general shook his head.

'I do not understand.'

'A man came here before me. Where is he?'

'No man. We see no man.'

Simon might have spoken then, but the uncomplimentary epithet which Tanya had attached to his name made him reticent. Besides, just at that moment one of the Chinese civilians let out a yelp, pointing at the well. The Saint let the taut rope slip quickly through his hands, dropping him from the sight of those above ground. As he descended he could hear Tanya's voice above the others.

'What is it?'

'Man in well,' the general translated.

Simon could not distinguish any more words in the confusion of sounds that echoed in the depths of the well. He did not particularly care; he was much more interested in avoiding being trapped and possibly shot like a fish in a barrel. He could only hope that a theory he had formed in the afternoon would turn out to be right: he believed that an underground stream ran under the monastery, passing through the well, under the kitchen, and directly beside the liqueur-making vault.

Letting go the rope entirely, he dropped down into the water and found footing on the slippery bottom, bracing himself against the curving wall. To his relief, he felt that the water, which reached above his waist, was flowing and not still. Though his pistol had been submerged and possibly put out of commission, his breast pocket flashlight was in working order.

No rain of bullets was yet descending upon his head, but he moved quickly anyway. His feeble light showed him that his hopes of a tunnel carrying the water were better than confirmed: the channel seemed to have been artificially enlarged, possibly centuries before, at its downstream exit from the well—the direction which led towards the kitchen and the basement he had seen in the afternoon.

Inside the narrow passage the water level was higher than in the well, but there was still room for a man's head and shoulders above the surface. Undoubtedly the monks of older, more generally dangerous times, had used the tunnel for some such purpose as the Saint was using it now, and it seemed likely that in their anxiety and eagerness to escape from irreverent barons or rampaging Protestants they would have provided a more private means of entrance and exit than the well in the middle of their courtyard.

Simon moved on with the flowing water until he saw a glimmer of light. It was not, however, the door he had hoped for. Putting his eye to the glowing chink in the wall he found that he was standing just outside the basement he had visited earlier in the day. He could see the rows of bottles and tiers of casks. Then he saw Tanya and the general coming into the basement from the foot of the steps, Tanya's pistol still pointed at the nape of the general's neck. The Saint postulated that either she was pulling a good bluff or that Igor and Ivan had shown themselves and taken control in the courtyard.

'And where are the real monks?' she was asking.

'In heaven, of course,' the general replied, with successful irony in spite of his bad pronunciation. 'They were ready. Graves already dug.'

'Where are the devices made?'

The general was not so co-operative in response to that inquiry.

'Speak,' she said, 'or I shoot.'

'They are made here,' he said.

'Where?'

The general made a resigned gesture of his shoulders and hands.

'I show you. You see. I push this first.'

Tanya aimed the pistol more carefully and tightened her finger on the trigger.

'Slowly,' she cautioned.

The general nodded and pressed something on which a wooden ladle was hanging. There was an electric humming, then a rumbling sound as the central sections of the two longest walls of the chamber began pivoting. The place was transformed, as the shelves of dusty bottles swung out of sight, into an entirely modern workshop. The newly revealed sides of the walls were lined with work benches and shelves covered with electronic components, chemicals, precision tools—and large numbers of the familiar exploding transistor radios and lighter-cameras.

'Give me samples of the micro-explosive and the formula for it before we destroy this place.'

The general did not move.

'I destroy you also unless you give me the formula,' Tanya said. 'You have tried to kill me many times. It would not seem unfair for me to kill you once.'

'I give,' said the general.

He pointed to a large chest.

'There.'

'Get it,' Tanya told him.

As she turned to keep her gun on the general, arms reached suddenly from draperies and grabbed her, knocking aside the gun, and throwing her on to the floor out of the Saint's field of view.

He moved swiftly further down the tunnel, searching for a connection between the passage and the monastery vaults. Within twenty paces he found it: a small door with a circle of pocked iron which served as a handle. Bracing his feet he put all his strength into the pull. The hinges seemed to be rusted solid, but their fastenings were so old that they gave way and bent soundlessly.

Simon stepped into the dryness and warmth of a small unlighted room crowded with crates and piles of cardboard cartons. He did not need his flashlight, for the door of the room was half open, letting through enough indirect illumination to allow him to find his way quietly around the heaps of boxes. There was a fire extinguisher and an axe on the wall by the door, and overhead like a tangle of snakes ran a thick bundle of electric cables. This was obviously not one of those rooms open to tourists.

He realized immediately, as he got a look into the main basement through dark curtains just slightly parted at the doorway, that he was standing in the exact spot where Tanya's captor had stood to grab her. The General and two other uniformed Chinese, their backs towards the Saint, held pistols on Tanya.

'Drop your guns,' Simon said, thinking it best to communicate his wishes in the simplest possible English.

At the same time, he stuck his automatic through the curtains. When the Chinese had dropped their pistols to the floor he showed himself.

'If you think you're surprised, Tanya, dear, you should have seen my face when you showed up.'

Before she could reply, the general let out a desperate shout, and the two other men dived for Simon. It would have been a suicidal move on their part except for one thing: when the Saint pulled the trigger of his automatic it emitted only a sodden click. He was hurled back against the wall, his head glancing against the stones.

When his vision cleared a moment later the Chinese were once more in control, holding their dry pistols on him and Tanya.

'You are interested in our work, and you have seen,' the general said. 'Now we take you back upstairs and kill you.'

'Where are Ivan and Igor?' the Saint asked Tanya.

'Quiet,' snapped the general.

But, looking at Tanya, Simon saw her give a kind of answer with an upward roll of her eyes.

The general opened a big refrigerator and checked the contents—rows of small amber bottles.

'You not take anything from here?' he asked Simon.

'No.'

The general went on counting. When he closed the door again he looked satisfied.

'Explosive,' he said. 'Fuses must be cold.' He nodded towards the wood-burning heater, which showed orange flame through its grill. 'Heat make explosion. Very big.'

Then he set into operation the mechanism that pivoted the walls, and half a minute later the chamber had once more become the dusty home of Grand Abrouillac.

'Now,' the general said, pointing into the side room through which Simon had come. 'This way.'

As they went through the curtains and passed the threshold, Simon whispered to Tanya, 'Scream your head off. Now!'

She screamed with enough force to frighten a banshee, furnishing an instant of confusion which was all the Saint needed. He toppled a pile of cartons towards the guards, snatched the fire axe from the wall, and sank the heavy blade into the mass of electric cables. The wooden handle insulated him from the spectacular multiplicity of short circuits which resulted. Sparks exploded over the room as the light bulbs went off, and in the weird flashing brilliance Simon was able to see enough to swing his medieval weapon again with deadly accuracy.

Both guards went down, and Tanya, who had crouched to escape the whistling blade, grabbed one of their pistols. The sparks were dying, and the general had plunged back into the pitch darkness of the liqueur-making vault. The fine beam of Simon's light caught him as he felt his way to the foot of the stairs.

Tanya fired, and the general sprawled heavily forward on to the stone floor. Instantly there was a tremendous fusillade of gunfire at ground level outside.

'Ivan and Igor!' Tanya cried, and bolted up the stairs. 'They were guarding the Chinese upstairs.'

'Stay inside!' Simon called after her.

He had stooped by the general's body. Now he followed her up to the door and stopped her before she could unbolt it. But already the outburst of shots was dwindling. As the Saint pushed Tanya back and opened the door himself he heard only three scattered reports, and then no more.

Igor leaned against the wall a few feet away, clutching a bloody arm. Ivan came running up, automatic in hand, calling anxious questions in Russian.

As Smolenko answered, Simon looked over the moonlit courtyard, where bodies lay scattered over the ancient ground like fallen puppets. It was fairly obvious that Igor and Ivan had been distracted momentarily by Tanya's shot, and their prisoners had gone for their own guns. The Russians, sheltered by shadows and the stone archways of the cloisters while their enemies were caught in the open, had won the battle, and all the Chinese, with Anton, lay dead.

'I never thought I'd be glad to see you two,' Simon said to Ivan and Igor.

'I'm afraid this will change your mind.'

It was Tanya speaking, and she aimed her pistol at his chest. Calm but puzzled, he looked at her.

'I don't understand,' he said levelly.

'Molière told them before they killed him—about your real mission.'

'My real mission? I'm sincerely curious to know what that is.'

'To use me until you had found the micro-explosive, and then to dispose of us and steal the formula yourself.'

Simon shook his head.

'Molière was just trying to save his skin.'

Tanya's voice was louder.

'You used me. Made me a fool. But now it no longer matters. Ivan and Igor received orders from higher—to kill you. Now we shall have the explosive and you shall not have even your life. Ivan, go below and bring up samples. The formula may be in a chest beside the refrigerator.'

'Sorry to disappoint you, Colonel,' Simon said, 'but nobody gets the formula.'

'What do you mean?'

'No electricity. The movable walls are jammed solid.'

'Ivan. Wait.' She thought for a second. 'We repair the wires.'

'No time. Remember the refrigerator full of fuses and explosives? The cooling has stopped, but that wood-burning monster of a stove is still going full blast. It would take several hours to untangle and match up and reconnect all those melted wires, and by that time this place will have been transformed into picturesque ruins.'

'You planned this, so we could not get the formula!'

'I must admit that the thought did pass through my

mind. On the other hand, remember that I won't get it either.'

Tanya's face twisted into an expression of hatred. She lowered the pistol and slapped him again and again. He did not flinch, but his eyes narrowed.

'I dare you to do that without your army around.'

'You swine! You lied—cheated me.'

Igor raised his pistol.

'We have orders. I kill him.'

'No,' Tanya said. 'He is mine. Go.'

The men hesitated.

'Go, I say. Have Igor's arm attended to. Prepare the car and my luggage.'

Ivan and Igor left the courtyard by the main gates. Simon leaned back against the wall and waited as Tanya turned to confront him. Even in the moonlight he could not make out the nuances of her expression.

'Isn't the condemned man allowed a last request?' he asked lightly.

Tanya did not answer, only waited, holding the gun on him as the ponderous footsteps of Ivan and Igor receded down the path.

'It's usually a cigarette,' the Saint said, 'but since I've given up smoking, how about a kiss? In memory of old times.'

'I could never come so close,' she said slowly. 'I understand that it would be deadly to touch with my gun anybody so skilled in the arts of self-defence as you.'

'You never can tell,' he said.

For several seconds they faced one another without speaking as clouds scudded across the face of the moon, and rising winds gave a voice to the forest.

Then Tanya stepped forward and placed the barrel of her pistol against his chest.

He pushed the cold steel aside and pulled her body close, kissing her deeply.

'You will have to make it seem real,' she whispered. 'Hit me hard, and then run. They may be waiting near. Can you go over the wall?'

'There's a door from the kitchen to the outside. I saw it this afternoon. I'll take your gun and shoot the lock if necessary.'

He took her face in his hands and forced her to look him in the eyes.

'The door's big enough for two, and there's a big world on the other side of it.'

'I . . . I'm afraid that is quite impossible. Maybe . . .'

'Later?'

'Later. Perhaps. But now . . . hit me after I fire one shot.'

'Goodbye, comrade.'

'Goodbye.'

She fired the pistol into one of the crumbling arches. Simon hit her, just hard enough, and caught her in his arms as her knees buckled and her gun dropped to the ground. He lowered her gently, smoothed the soft brown hair from her face, and walked swiftly from the courtyard into the kitchen. The outer door was padlocked, but a single shot freed it.

Striding and sliding down the pathless mountainside, he felt a bittersweet mixture of sadness and relief. He paused and looked back up at the hulk of old stone almost lost to his sight among the moon-touched firs. Then he turned, measured the weight of the general's purse of gold coins, which had by some mysterious means found its way into his Saintly pocket, and went on down once more for a while to the world of ordinary things.

THE SAINT . . .

. . . "that amiable rascal" *Sunday Times*

. . . "that happy inspiration" *Scotsman*

. . . "that exhilarating character" *Liverpool Post*

. . . "has become an institution" *The Observer*